There was no denying something had developed between them, but what was that something?

If this was love, then it was a quiet comfort, riding side by side with an excitement deep inside, unlike anything she'd ever felt before. She tried to ask God for an answer, but she kept getting too distracted by the warmth of Garrett's hand as he walked beside her.

Or was this what it was like to be, as the classic phrase said, "caught on the rebound"? She'd often heard the phrase but never understood it. Now, here she was, walking through the forest holding hands with a man she had only just met, when a week ago she wore another man's engagement ring. And she'd just kissed him, too. Not just a friendly peck kind of kiss, but the kind that made a woman's insides melt.

A week. The thought echoed through her brain. What was she doing? Had she lost her mind?

The path widened to the opening onto the road through the campground. A week. They talked of love, and she'd known him a week. And on vacation, yet, not even a normal life-style setting. What was she doing?

She pulled her hand out of his.

GAIL SATTLER was born and raised in Winnipeg, Manitoba, and now lives in Vancouver, B.C. (where you don't have to shovel rain) with her husband, three sons, dog, and countless fish, many of whom have names. Gail became a Christian with her husband after he joined AA. She began writing when the company she worked for closed and she chose to stay home with her children. She writes inspirational romance because she loves happily-ever-afters and believes God has a place in that happy ending. She now works part-time as office manager for a web design company.

Books by Gail Sattler

HEARTSONG PRESENTS
HP269—Walking the Dog
HP306—Piano Lessons

Gone Camping

Gail Sattler

Heartsong Presents

To my husband Tim, and my kids Justin, Chris, and Tyrone, who make camping so much fun.

A note from the author:
I love to hear from my readers! You may correspond with me by writing: **Gail Sattler**
Author Relations
PO Box 719
Uhrichsville, OH 44683

ISBN 1-57748-550-5

GONE CAMPING

Cover illustration by Victoria Lisi and Julius.

PRINTED IN THE U.S.A.

one

Roberta ignored the pounding at the front door as she blew her nose.

Molly's muffled voice was accompanied by more pounding. "Robbie, Robbie! I know you're home. Please, let me in!"

Roberta glanced at the clock and wondered why Molly wasn't at work. Despite her red-rimmed eyes and blotchy face, Roberta opened the door. Immediately, Molly threw her arms around her.

"Oh, Robbie!" she moaned, "I just heard what happened! You didn't answer your phone, so I came over as fast as I could."

Just when she thought she had herself under control, Roberta started to sob again. "Today I discovered for myself that the rumors were true." Tears streamed down her cheeks. She made no effort to wipe them.

Molly hugged her tighter. "How did you find out?"

After a few more stifled sobs, Roberta managed to continue. "I went to work early to surprise Mike, but I was the one who got the surprise. Mike and Suzie were in the corner of the stockroom. . .and they were. . ." Roberta gulped, trying to sniffle back more tears while fighting for the right words. "I didn't even say anything; I turned and ran. Like a fool I hid in the washroom and bawled my eyes out. Mike stormed in, and the whole office heard his rampage. Then this was waiting for me on my desk." She thrust the crumpled piece of company letterhead at her friend.

Molly stared at it, mouthing the words as she read.

Dear Miss Garland:
This letter is to inform you that effective immediately, your services are no longer required.

Enclosed is your final check. Your vacation pay, other monies owed to you, and letter of recommendation for your years of service will be forwarded by post.

Good luck in future endeavors.

Regards,
Michael Flannigan, Sr.
President

Molly slowly handed her back the letter. "So. The wedding's off, and his dad fired you. . ."

All Roberta could do was nod as the tears threatened to break through again. As a Christian, she valued trust above all else in a relationship. Not only did Mike obviously not feel the same, but he had betrayed her in the worst way.

"When I arrived to pick you up for lunch and Suzie said you no longer worked there, I thought it was a joke, except no one was smiling. Then I asked what Mike thought about it, and she just laughed." Molly clasped her hands in front of her. "Oh, Robbie, I don't know what to say. But if it makes you feel better, the receptionist told me Mike didn't deserve you anyway."

"Thanks," Roberta sniffled. Not that it helped.

"You don't have to put up with that treatment, you know." Molly crossed her arms. "They can't fire you. You can take them to court."

Roberta shook her head. "What for? To get my job back? I loved my job, but how could I ever face those people again? And how could I work beside Mike or his father?" Roberta sniffed again, lowering her voice. "Or Suzie. I'll get another job. On my way out, Michael Senior said he would give me a considerable severance package. Life goes on."

"I know!" Molly exclaimed, raising one finger in the air. "You need to get away from all this. A change of scenery. You need a vacation!"

Roberta wiped her eyes with her sleeve. "I'm unemployed. I can't afford a vacation. While I don't think I'll go looking for another job tomorrow, I doubt that I'm going to be taking a wild vacation."

"No, not a wild vacation. After work tomorrow I'm going camping with Gwen and her twin brother for a week. Do you want to come? Their tent trailer has three double beds in it, but I'm sure Garrett won't want to spend the night under the same roof as us girls anyway. It'll be fun."

Roberta shook her head. "Me? No, I'm not going to tag along with you and your friends."

"Don't be silly. You're my friend, so naturally you're their friend, too. You remember them, don't you?"

Roberta was silent as she thought for a minute. Certainly she would have remembered friends of Molly's that were twins. "Sorry, I don't think so."

"We were planning on meeting Garrett at the campground."

"Why in the world would you want him along? Is there something going on between you two that I don't know about? And does your friend mind her brother coming?"

Molly shook her head. "No, nothing like that. It was Gwen's suggestion. Maybe he has some time off work or something. He's really good-looking and very nice, but not my type."

Roberta backed up a step. "I don't want to tag along. I think I'll just stay at home, thanks."

Molly snorted. "Not a chance, Robbie. In fact, I insist. Not only that, you can help us. If you took the camper tonight, then we'd be assured of a great spot for our week's vacation. No reservations, first come, first served. So you can be the first one there!"

Roberta almost visualized the gears whirring in Molly's head. She held her hands up, palms facing Molly, in an attempt to ward her off. "You can't make me do that. You know I've never been camping in my life. Besides, if I went tonight, that would mean I would be out there all alone. No way!"

Molly made a calculated laughing sound. "You won't be alone. Garrett will be there."

Shaking her head furiously, Roberta didn't drop her raised

hands. "Oh, no. I'm not spending the night in the middle of nowhere with a strange man keeping watch over me. You've conned me too many times for me to get sucked in like that. Not this time. No way. I'm staying home."

"He's not strange. I've known him for years."

Roberta noticed Molly's lack of reference to everything else she mentioned. "No."

Molly shrugged her shoulders. "How about if I spent the night with you?"

Roberta dropped her hands to her side. "What?"

"The campground is only an hour's drive out of town. I could be there in time for a late supper if you pick up the groceries. How about it?"

"No."

"We can have a wienie roast, just you and me."

"Really? Uh, I don't know. . ."

"Hurry up; I have to be back at work in a few minutes."

"But I don't think—"

"We'll have a great time. . ."

"But I—"

"Going, going. . ."

Roberta raised her hands up, then slapped them to her sides. "Oh, all right! I'll go!"

"Great!" Molly shouted and clapped her hands. "I'll tell you everything you need to know." She reached into her purse and handed Roberta her key ring. "Here. Drive me to work."

"What? Why?"

"So you can go get the camper. My car has a hitch. Yours doesn't, does it?"

Roberta laughed for the first time that day. "Of course not."

"Let's go. I'll tell you how to set it up on the way there. It's important to do everything in the right order. Maybe you should write, and I'll drive."

"How are you going to get home?"

"With Gwen. We can only have two cars parked on the spot, so the only two cars we can use are mine and hers."

That answered that. Kind of. While Molly drove back to her office, Roberta tried desperately to write down Molly's rush of instructions, a near impossibility in the moving vehicle.

"Sleeping bags are already in it. Bring your own pillow. See you about sundown. Bye!"

Roberta smiled hesitantly as Molly raced out the car door and disappeared into the entrance of the office tower. Why did she have the feeling she was making a big mistake?

ஓ

Roberta experimented with the brakes, testing the added weight of the full trailer behind her before she had to come to a stop in real traffic. She sucked in a deep breath and willed her hands to stop shaking. She could do this.

All the way down the highway, despite strict adherence to the posted speed limit, she could see the lineup of cars behind her. Every time another irritated driver whizzed past, she tightened her already iron grip on the steering wheel. When at last she arrived at the park entrance gate, she heaved a sigh of relief.

Slowly, she bumped down the gravel road to the designated camping area, where she used her best judgment to pick one of the many large sites still available. A sign instructed campers to pick a spot; a park ranger would register it later.

One day she would get Molly back for this.

Stopping the car and trailer a little beyond the entrance to the site, she mentally prepared to back in. With no one to help direct her, she desperately tried to remember Molly's rapid-fire list of instructions during the ten-minute drive back to work. All Roberta could remember were cautions to steer the opposite way when backing up. And Molly's friend's mother had warned her something about "jackknifing." She'd heard it mentioned in reference to the big highway trucks, but never knew what it meant.

On the bright side, no one was around to laugh if she did it wrong. However, at some point, someone would come by, and she was blocking the one-way gravel road.

Roberta craned her neck to examine the wide opening one last time, sucked in a deep breath, and shifted into reverse. After considerable manipulation, she managed to back up most of the way into the spot, but the trailer was crooked and too close to the picnic table. At least she didn't hit it.

Her second and third attempts were worse.

She dropped her forehead to the steering wheel with a bump. Why did she say she was going to do this? Why did she have to get there when Gwen and Garrett's mother was already late for an appointment? The woman had thrown her a massive set of keys, told her how to release the pin lock, helped her hook the trailer to the back of Molly's car, and had driven off, leaving Roberta in the driveway.

Roberta pressed her forehead into the steering wheel and drew in a deep breath. After one more attempt, if the trailer was still crooked, she would give up and leave it where it was, even if it was on top of the fire pit.

"Hi there," a pleasant baritone voice resounded from beside the door. "Need some help, miss?"

Roberta rolled her head on the steering wheel and raised her eyes to see a man standing outside the open window, smiling at her. She raised her head to see him better. His green base-ball cap bore the emblem of the Parks and Recreation Division, and together with a pair of large dark sunglasses, the overall effect shielded most of his face. Below the sunglasses, he had the nicest smile she had ever seen. A khaki-colored shirt bearing a crest with the same emblem as the hat accompanied baggy black shorts, which showed off strong hairy legs. Beat-up hiking boots with wool work socks sticking above the rim completed the picture of a rugged park ranger.

Unwilling to make another attempt at failure, she thought about his offer. Molly said any of the park rangers would be able to help if Garrett was unavailable, and since she had no idea what Garrett looked like, who he was, or what time he would be there, the offer of help from a ranger was too good to pass up.

"At the risk of looking like a helpless female, I've never pulled a trailer before, much less backed one in. I appear to be doing something wrong."

The ranger grinned, showing off some rather attractive dimples and a flashing white row of straight teeth. Sunlight glinted off the frames of the dark sunglasses, emphasizing the deep tone of his skin. For a split second, Roberta considered him very attractive and wished she could see his eyes. But then, her better judgment took over. It would be a long time before she would even look at a man again.

"You've never driven with a trailer before? I could never tell." His smile widened.

Roberta scowled back.

He rested one hand on the mirror. "If you want, I could back it in for you."

Roberta narrowed her eyes to think about it. The man was a park ranger, after all, not a petty hoodlum about to steal Molly's car. And she was obviously doing a poor job herself. She met his eyes and forced a smile. "Yes, please." As she got out of the car, she couldn't help but notice how tall he was as he passed her on his way in.

The ranger bumped his knees against the steering wheel before reaching down to adjust the seat in order to position both long hairy legs underneath the steering wheel. He drove forward to straighten the trailer out, then backed it in smoothly, positioning it perfectly with the first effort.

He stepped out and tipped his hat. "Will that be all, miss?" he asked, smiling at her again.

Roberta dared not ask him to help unhitch it. After all, she had her notes. "Thank you very much. I appreciate your help, but I think I can manage on my own from here."

"Very well," he replied. Holding the brim of his cap, he straightened it on his head. "See you after you're settled so we can get you registered." He smiled again and left.

Roberta checked her notes.

Her list said to block it, support it, and unhook it. She stared at the trailer, still attached to Molly's car. That had sounded so simple while Molly barked out instructions. A few pieces of wood had surrounded the tires in the driveway, so she did the same.

Roberta stood back to admire the start of her project. Molly had mentioned something about legs under the trailer, so Roberta lowered herself gently in the gravel to her hands and knees and pulled down four spring-loaded contraptions, one tucked in each corner, and adjusted them until they touched the ground.

According to the list, the next step was to unhitch it, so she started turning the crank to raise the hooking thingie above the hitch. Nothing moved. She cranked and cranked until she started to sweat and stopped. Roberta swiped a sheen of moisture off her brow, needing to take a breather. When she stood back, she noticed a clip on top of the locking mechanism. Roberta narrowed her eyes and scowled at it. What a stupid place to put a safety latch.

She fought with it until her fingers were sore, and finally it released. After flexing her numb fingers, she started cranking again. Finally, using considerable effort, she had barely worked it high enough to drive Molly's car forward when she heard the same baritone voice behind her.

"Hi, how's it going, miss?" he said cheerfully.

Roberta felt far from cheerful. She was sweaty, her fingers were sore, and her shoulders ached from all that cranking. And while she was thinking of cranking, she felt *cranky*.

"Fine," she replied curtly. Standing straight, she realized she should try to be pleasant. Even though she was getting nowhere fast, if the ranger was back, then he probably thought she should have finished setting up by now, and she still didn't even have the car pulled away. She couldn't read the expression behind the ranger's dark glasses, but she thought he was frowning.

"I think you should have a piece of wood under there, or you're going to find it will sink in the gravel."

Roberta sagged. A piece of wood? After all the work and sweat, she was going to have to do this all over again? She squeezed her eyes shut, and in the back of her mind, she recalled seeing a piece of wood under the pin in the driveway.

"Oh," was her only reply.

The ranger studied her, making her feel even dumber. "Want me to do it for you? I see you've already been working hard at it." It might have been her imagination, but Roberta thought he was struggling to keep a straight face.

At work, she only ever lifted a few books and light boxes. For someone so badly out of shape, cranking the trailer up was hard work, and she was sorry it showed.

The thought of her ex-job froze her where she stood. Thanks to Mike, the ex-love of her life, she was now unemployed. She could still barely believe his father defended his conduct by firing her.

The more she thought about it, the more she realized she should have figured it out. Instances started to pop into her mind, making her realize that everyone, including Mike's father, knew what was going on and hid it from her. Naively, she had ignored every hint of any indiscretion, listened to every one of his many excuses, refusing to believe Mike was anything less than loyal and happily in love with her. For a while, he'd even started to attend church with her.

Roberta looked back at the ranger, who had been watching her the entire time she stared off into space. What she really wanted was to be left alone. If she treated him politely and answered him, maybe he would go away.

"That would be nice, thank you very much. I guess I'm more out of shape than I thought." She forced herself to smile graciously.

With no apparent effort, the ranger turned the crank, easily lifting the shaft off the ground, slid in the piece of wood, then cranked it up high enough to clear the ball and drive forward.

Roberta noticed the ease with which he turned it. She hopped in the car, drove forward a few yards, parked it, and returned just as the ranger cranked the trailer back down to the right spot.

"You know, my family has this same kind of tent trailer, and it gets hard to turn the crank at exactly the same spot. How about that?" He smiled again at her.

Roberta gritted her teeth. The last thing she felt like doing was making conversation with a strange man alone in the middle of nowhere. She did not smile back. "Thank you very much. I think I can handle it myself from here."

He nodded, tipped his hat again, and strode out of the campsite. Roberta assumed he would continue making his rounds.

Checking her notes, the next step was to crank the roof of the tent up. She dragged her hand over her face at the thought of more cranking. How did she ever let Molly con her again?

She tried every key on the key chain, and finally the last one fit in the lock for the storage compartment. Finding another crank, she inserted it into the slot at the back of the trailer and went back to work.

After turning forever, the roof finally reached the top. Her back ached, so she stretched her arms above her head to try to release the kinks, then resigned herself to the next step. According to the list, she had to pull out the beds and insert the support bars.

Roberta emptied bazillions of poles from the storage compartment, then sorted them into piles. With her head bent and hands on her hips, she tried to figure out what in the world they would be for. Unable to, she skimmed the list with her finger, hoping a name for their uses would help her match them up. About halfway down the paper, standing in the midst of the poles in neat piles about her feet, she heard that same voice again.

"Hi. Making any progress?"

Her finger still on the paper, she raised her head to see the ranger again, standing a few feet away, his long legs slightly spread and planted firmly, his hands resting on his hips, a clipboard held loosely in the crook of one arm. He wore an annoyingly smug smile on his face, but his lips were pressed together tightly, like he was trying not to laugh.

She said nothing as she glared at him, waiting for him to say something.

"You've never done this before, have you?"

Roberta blushed. If only there had been more time for Molly to give her better instructions. If only Molly's friend's mother hadn't been in such a rush to get going. If only she had told Molly to forget this dumb idea and stayed home. "No, I haven't. It's not mine."

"Ah," he mused, tapping the end of his pen against his cheek, the other hand still resting on one hip, holding the clipboard. "Like I said earlier, my family has one just like this. Want me to help you set it up? There's hardly anyone here, and I think I can spare the time."

"Look, I appreciate your concern, but I really can do this myself. If you really want to help, how about if you tell me which poles go where, and I can do the rest."

His chin lowered almost imperceptibly as his smile faded. Finally he was getting the hint. "Of course." The clipboard remained in the crook of one arm, and he pointed with the pen to the various piles as he spoke. "The ones with the flat ends support the pullouts, and the ones with the small round ends go inside to hold up the tent on top of the beds, those are for the awning, and those look like they're for a tent, which you don't appear to have with you. Are you sure you want to do this by yourself?"

"Yes, thank you very much." Try as she might, she couldn't keep the sharp edge out of her voice. Mike had always insisted on doing everything for her, expecting her to be grateful, when all it did was make her feel useless, then guilty for not appreciating him. This ranger was not going to make her feel the same.

He nodded and left again, this time not tipping his hat.

Roberta heaved and pulled, struggling to pull the beds out,

then wiggled and manipulated the poles until everything was securely supported. For a moment she admired her work, then pulled the list out of her pocket. She eyed the poles that the ranger said held up the sides by the beds. However, the list said that the next step was to insert the door.

Roberta froze. Insert the door? What door? She ran her hand along the door-sized opening in the side and dragged her palm down her face.

She finally located the door on the bed inside the trailer. Delicately, she gave it an experimental push and discovered it was heavier than it looked. The top of the frame showed a series of slots, and the bottom of the frame had a few clips to hold it in place. Now to get it there.

She picked it up, tipping it awkwardly to try to fit it into place. The harder she tried to fit it in, the heavier it became. Then, just as she thought she had it, it slipped. Roberta jerked her knee upward to prevent it from crashing to the floor, smashing it into her kneecap.

"Are you all right?"

That voice again. Mr. Ranger was back.

Roberta looked up, bringing herself face-to-face with a large pair of dark sunglasses and a big bright smile.

Her knee stung. "I'll live, thank you. Nothing's damaged." Except her pride. Her temper was working overtime though.

"Want me to do that for you?"

Without a word, she grumpily handed him the heavy door and stepped out of the trailer opening. Of course he showed no indication of it being heavy. He effortlessly slotted it into the holes, gave it a little push, and fitted it neatly into the bottom of the frame in seconds flat. Fastening it to the bottom half of the door, he never lost that insipid smile. Roberta glared back.

"There! Done." He wiped his hands on the back of his shorts. His smile faded quickly as he saw her grumpy face. "Well, call me if you need any more help." And he left again.

Roberta stomped outside to the picnic table where she had left the list. It was gone.

Since the campsite was almost completely surrounded by trees, Roberta assumed it had to have blown off the table. The bright white of the paper would contrast with the darkness of the ground cover, making it easy to find. Walking a bit farther into the trees, she paused to inhale a deep breath of fresh air.

Somewhere in the forest, squirrels chattered and birds chirped. The wind rustled the leaves, and in the distance, Roberta could hear children laughing, playing at some far-off campsite. A slight breeze carried the pleasant scent of a campfire and burnt hamburgers. Roberta smiled.

Despite the trouble she'd had so far in setting up, Roberta considered the possibility that maybe Molly was right. Getting away from the city into the peaceful surroundings of the campground could go a long way to helping her sort things out.

On her quest to find the missing list, Roberta glanced upward, searching for a glimpse of the nearby squirrel, chattering away as it sat in the high branches. As she walked, her sandal caught in a branch on the ground, and she lost her balance. She flailed her arms but couldn't stop herself, and she hit the ground with a thud. Pain shot through her already sore knee as it struck a jagged rock, and her arm scraped against a branch, leaving a painful stinging welt.

Roberta lay facedown on the ground, in total disbelief at all that had gone wrong. Maybe this camping business wasn't such a good idea after all.

Lying inelegantly sprawled on the ground, she considered standing up, except that surely something else would go wrong. On the other hand, if she continued to lie in the dirt long enough, maybe she would wake up and find this had all been a bad dream. She let her mind wander. Maybe she could get comfortable down here among the rocks and branches. She could have a nap if some rabid chipmunk didn't come along and bite her.

Footsteps. Running. No, anything but that.

"Miss! Miss! Are you all right!?"

Not Mr. Ranger again! Roberta pushed herself up on her

hands and knees, barely managing to put any weight on her left leg without her knee buckling. She rubbed the scratch on her arm, which was bleeding slightly. She couldn't keep the bite out of her voice as she spoke.

"Look, I just tripped. Nothing serious. Thank you for your concern, but I really want to be alone, okay?"

"I was concerned when you didn't get up."

"I'm fine!" she snapped. "Now why don't you just go away!" She glared at him, trying her best to get him to take a hint.

Instead of leaving, Mr. Ranger stood in one spot, his lower lip quivering, like he was trying to stifle a smile. Roberta couldn't see what he was looking at behind his dark glasses.

"Okay, fine," he mumbled. Again, he turned and left.

She neared the boiling point. The last thing she needed was for Mr. Ranger to laugh at her. This camping stuff was more trouble than it was worth. She reached up to push her hair back off her forehead when her fingers came in contact with a hard object. Her fingers gripped it, and she pulled out a stick, along with a number of strands of her hair.

With a growl, Roberta broke the stick into small pieces and threw them on the ground, grinding them up with her foot. How did she let Molly convince her to do this?

If it wasn't for Mike, she would be sitting at her desk, calmly working away in an air-conditioned office. The thought of her job made her even angrier. Life wasn't fair! She had been fired because her fiancé was fooling around on her, yet there was nothing she could do about it.

Roberta limped back to the camper. Her knee ached and her arm stung, but she was too angry to care. She was going to get this stupid thing set up without the instructions or die trying. She slammed the poles on the ground into one pile, then lugged them into the camper and threw them on one of the beds, the poles clanging loudly as they bounced together.

As she sat on the bed, she figured out how they fitted in and fought with them until everything slid into place. With everything done, Roberta struggled with the middle bed, changing it back into the table. Finally done, Roberta stood in the center of the trailer and heaved a sigh of relief. Success.

A nice cup of coffee would really hit the spot, despite the heat of the summer afternoon. She frowned as she examined the propane-powered elements. She had not hooked up the propane tank connection, and the bed and support bars were over the propane tank. Now she would have to crawl under the overhang where it would be awkward. Why not? Everything else had gone wrong.

Cringing with every movement, Roberta crawled underneath the bed, hunched beneath the overhang, and tried to ignore the gravel digging into her as she proceeded to screw the hose onto the tank. Not wanting to take chances with the connection, she decided to exchange the screwdriver for a wrench, if she could find one. A map to locate all the little cubbyholes and compartments in this thing would have been handy.

When Roberta started to back out from her cramped work space, her poor knee couldn't take the contact with the hard gravel. Straightening up a bit too soon, she hit her head on the overhang.

Biting her lip, she heard a sound from a few feet away. Holding her head, she backed out the rest of the way, and turning around, came face-to-face with good old Mr. Ranger again. It was apparent that he sincerely tried to suppress the urge to laugh, but he didn't do it very well.

"What do you want now?" she barked at him, still holding her head.

He evidently managed to control himself; his mouth straightened as he said, "Let's get you registered. And have you got that propane properly connected? I see you don't have a wrench there. It may not be tight enough."

Roberta reached the end of her rope. Her disastrous morning. Molly railroading her into this idiotic camping trip. The nerve-wracking drive. The trouble setting up. And every time she turned around, there was Mr. Ranger, always showing up whenever she did something stupid or clumsy. And here he was again, telling her something she already knew. Of course she needed a wrench. She wasn't brain-dead.

She knew the Bible spoke of patience, but not a single verse came to mind. "I know I need a wrench!" She waved her hands in the air as she hollered at him. "I just have to find out where it is! I was going to do that when you barged in on me again. Don't you have something better to do? Some wild animals to document or something?"

Mr. Ranger frowned and stepped backward. "Sor–ry!" he exclaimed sarcastically. "I'll sign you in and be out of your way." He flipped to the right page and held up his pen, ready to write. He cleared his throat. "Name and number of people in your party."

Roberta glared at him. "Roberta Garland. And the whole group won't be here until tomorrow."

He looked up with the frown still on his face. "You mean you're here alone for the night?"

"No, one friend will be here tonight, and two more the next night. I don't know how long everyone will be staying, including myself." She glared at him, wishing she could see his eyes beneath those dark glasses.

They glared at each other in silence.

"Look, I've got a wrench in the truck." He sighed. "I can make sure the propane hose is tight enough. I see you're limping. I can get some ice for that knee if you want."

Roberta scowled at him, but he said nothing. He only scowled back at her, looking like he was starting to lose his patience with her, too.

"I don't want your help. I don't want anyone's help!" Roberta screamed. "Coming out here like this wasn't my idea. I don't even care if I blow myself up anymore! Leave me alone!" Tears burned the back of her eyes.

Mr. Ranger stared at her. As his mouth gaped open, Roberta realized she had been taking all her hurt and anger and frustration out on this helpful stranger.

Her lower lip wouldn't stop quivering, making her feel like a fool. Unable to help herself, the tears that threatened earlier burst to the surface. "I'm sorry; I'm having a bad day. Please go away!" she sobbed, and ran into the camper, slammed the door, and threw herself on one of the beds, leaving poor Mr. Ranger standing by himself, pen still poised in midair.

She knew he could hear her crying through the canvas walls, but she didn't care. When she lifted her head to wipe her eyes, she peeked through the screened window to see him still standing in the middle of the campsite, looking around as if wondering what he should do. Hesitantly, he turned around and left. Roberta lowered her head and cried herself out.

When her tears were exhausted, Roberta wiped her face on her sleeve, feeling like an idiot for bursting into tears in front of poor Mr. Ranger. In addition to looking like a hysterical female, she never should have screamed at him like that. She clambered down off the bed and tried to distract herself by keeping busy, starting by making herself familiar with where everything was stowed inside the small tent trailer.

Feeling utterly useless and totally dejected, she sat at the small table, resting her elbows on the table, and buried her face in her hands. Absently, she twirled a lock of her hair in her fingers, and as her fingers ran past her ear, her hand froze. She placed a hand on each ear to discover one dangly earring still in place; the other ear held nothing. Roberta groaned. Not only were they her favorite earrings, they were a gift from Molly.

First she made a thorough search of Molly's car and then, remembering her struggle with the door, searched the floor of the camper with no success.

Sitting on the floor, gingerly rubbing her sore knee, she wondered if the earring had fallen off outside when she sorted the poles. She limped outside, carefully watching the gravel with every footstep, then sat and gently picked through the dirt. By now the earring could be partially covered by a rock or whatever else the gravel contained. She shuddered at the thought.

Finding nothing, she sat on the ground in silence. Looking around the campsite, she desperately tried to remember what she had done and where she had done it.

Suddenly she closed her eyes. The bushes. When she fell.

Roberta tried her best to pick a relatively clean spot, and proceeded to pick through the leaves and debris on the ground. As she diligently searched, she heard footsteps.

"Hi. I just thought I'd check and make sure you were okay."

Mr. Ranger. Again. She refused to look at him, not wanting him to see her red and puffy eyes or her shiny nose. "I'm fine, thank you," she sniffed, knowing she looked anything but. She wished from the depths of her soul that he would leave.

He didn't. "What's the matter? Lose something?"

Roberta considered giving up. "Yes, I lost an earring." She tried to think of some way to tell him to get lost, right along with her earring, but he got the next word in.

"Want me to help you look?" Without waiting for an answer, he squatted until he was hunkered down beside her. "What does it look like?" he asked cheerfully.

Roberta sighed. The sooner she located the missing earring, the sooner he would go away. "Just like this one." She sighed again, tipping her head and lifting her hair so he could see it.

"Okay, let's look for it." He picked through the ground cover, so she resumed her search as well.

"So when is your friend coming?" he asked politely as he meticulously picked through the dirt.

Roberta glared at him, but with his head lowered, she couldn't see his face behind the brim of his hat and large dark sunglasses. Why did he keep coming back? Was Mr. Ranger trying to pick her up? Was this how Mike had picked up other women when he claimed he was madly in love with her? The thought made her start to simmer again.

"Soon!" she snapped. Her movements became more abrupt, throwing the sticks and rocks farther than necessary as she recalled her most recent memory of Mike, in the corner of the storage room with Suzie, their lips locked together.

Not fully recovered from her last bout of crying, she struggled against the telltale constriction in the back of her throat. She dared not speak, for fear of losing control again, and she bit her bottom lip and held her breath to try to maintain some semblance of dignity. It didn't help. Another river of tears rushed down her cheek, but this time she managed to keep silent.

"Found it! Here you go!" Mr. Ranger raised his head as he reached out his hand to give her the earring.

As she met his gaze through his dark sunglasses, she watched his bright smile fade. With shaking hands, she took the earring from him. Just her luck, a tear dripped off her chin and landed on his wrist. He flinched, and she froze.

"Hey, are you all right?" he asked, his voice soft and gentle. "Will your boyfriend be here soon?"

Roberta squeezed her eyes shut. Boyfriend. The tears starting flowing harder. She had no boyfriend, and she planned never to have a boyfriend again. It wasn't worth the heartache.

"Why can't you go away and leave me alone?" she sobbed as she ran back into the camper, gasping for breath.

She cried for a while, and when she looked outside, Mr. Ranger was gone.

two

Ranger Lamont sat at the table at the park office, resting his feet on an empty chair. What a day! Up until today, this job had been a lot of fun, but now he'd had his first troublesome camper.

That lady in site 27 was a nutcase.

Originally, he had only been trying to help a first-time camper. Normally, he wouldn't have interfered, but she was obviously alone and totally inept. It was almost as if she had never even seen anyone set up a tent trailer before, let alone done it herself. And she looked like she could really use some assistance setting up her boyfriend's camper, although she kept insisting she could do it alone.

He wondered if she was perhaps trying to surprise her boyfriend, who she claimed was coming later. Most likely after the boyfriend finished work, he would be joining her for supper; after all, they were only about an hour's drive out of the city, and many people did that. He wondered if said boyfriend would appreciate her efforts. For her, it appeared monumental.

When she first started setting up, it seemed every time he came back to check her progress, things got worse instead of better. When he saw her lying on the ground not moving, he had almost been ready to call an ambulance.

Then when she started screaming at him, he was ready to call the funny farm. At about the point she ran into the trailer sobbing something about having a bad day, he decided to keep his distance.

He was more than willing to help a lady in distress, but at that point, this lady was more distressed than he cared to handle. Too bad, because he had the impression that she could use a friend. She seemed like a nice person, if a bit unstable.

He checked the time once more and decided to make the registration rounds again.

He shook his head. He sure hoped her boyfriend arrived soon.

❧

Roberta sipped her coffee as she organized the inside of the camper. She hoped Mr. Ranger wouldn't see her again. If Molly arrived before he returned to collect the money, she wouldn't have to face him.

In preparation for Molly's arrival, she rolled out the sleeping bags on the beds. For tonight, it would be only the two of them. Molly planned to go straight to her job from the campsite in the morning, which would leave Roberta alone all day. Now that the camper was all set up, she looked forward to a day in the great outdoors.

As she familiarized herself with the layout, she found where everything was stowed. She removed her pillow and the duffel bag with her clothes and toiletries from Molly's car and placed them on one of the beds, then hauled the cooler out of the trunk and dropped it beside the picnic table.

Molly had told Roberta the camping trip would be her treat, and not to worry about food beyond tonight's supper and tomorrow's breakfast, or any other details beyond getting a good spot and setting up. Her mission accomplished, she was now ready to cast her troubles away and relax.

One of the things she discovered while digging through the storage compartments was a hammock. She had never been in one before, and from what she saw on television, they appeared comfortable. Plenty of trees graced this campsite, so she had lots of choices where to tie it. She looked forward to curling up with a good book.

She tied it securely to a couple of large trees, then tugged on it as hard as she could to be sure it would support her weight. She stood back and pushed on one of the wooden crosspieces, watching as the hammock swayed and spun one complete revolution, making her wonder how she could climb on it without falling off. People actually slept in these things, but first they had to get on.

Carefully and hesitantly, with her book tucked under her chin, she grabbed the hammock, one hand on each side. With one knee braced on the far side, all she had to do was lift the other leg, hoist herself up onto her hands and knees, and then she could sink into the center and flip over onto her back. Once her other leg was off the ground she could balance her way in. No problem.

As she lifted her left leg, she rested her weight on her right hand. Roberta stiffened as she realized she was leaning too much weight on one side, making the hammock start to pitch. She tried to redistribute her weight, making the hammock swing the other way as she balanced precariously. Her fingers clenched as hard as she could onto the sides, both hands clinging to the top portion as she braced herself on one knee, the other leg hanging over the edge as the hammock continued to lean. The ground moved precariously.

To her horror, the hammock continued in a rolling motion, the whole thing happening in slow motion like some outtake in a B-grade movie. Roberta hung on for dear life.

The hammock picked up speed as it continued to turn in its rolling motion. Her foot lifted off the ground when the hammock pitched, flipping completely over. The book slipped out from under her chin and shot into the bushes at the same time as she landed on the ground under the hammock with a thud, flat on her back.

With the wind knocked out of her, Roberta gulped for air. It didn't hurt too bad, but she was unable to move as she struggled to breathe, staring up at the bottom of the hammock from her inelegant position on the ground.

Gravel crunched, increasing in volume, as the running footsteps came closer.

"Miss! Are you hurt!? Can you speak!?"

Roberta looked up. Way up. She considered the odd perspective her position granted her. First she stared at Mr.

Ranger's battered and worn hiking boots, then up the length of a pair of long hairy legs. She could see a dark shadow where the loose shorts circled each leg. A tight pair of lips accompanied by large dark sunglasses and a green hat peered down at her.

He hunkered down beside her. Reaching one hand out, he waited for her to respond and grasp it so he could pull her up.

Not a chance. Embarrassment worse than anything so far flooded her face as she lay on the ground, flat on her back, looking up at him. She ignored the pinch of gravel on her back and the scrapes on her bare legs. "I think I lost my book."

Mr. Ranger smiled down at her. "Ah. I thought I saw something fly up and land in the bushes as you went flying over. Do you need some help getting into your hammock?"

Roberta squeezed her eyes shut as she continued to lie, unmoving, on her back. He had seen her go sailing over the top of the hammock. This whole day could have been a nightmare, except the pain in her knee and the gravel digging into her back told her she was wide awake.

He reached out again, and this time, Roberta tried not to blush as Mr. Ranger helped her to her feet.

"I guess there must be a trick to it or something."

"You know, I've got a hammock exactly like this. Did you buy it at Hank's Outdoor Store on the corner of Third and Main?"

"No."

He shrugged his shoulders, smiling. At her answering frown, he turned his head toward the bushes. "Well, then, let's find your book, and I'll show you how to crawl in."

Roberta couldn't believe his arrogance. First he had a camper just like Molly's friend, and now he had a hammock exactly like this. Mike always did the same thing, always trying to impress her, but this time she refused to fall for it. Just because he was the park ranger didn't mean he was an expert at everything. She would have eventually figured things out for herself, and she didn't need or want his help.

Without speaking, she started to search for her book. No way was she going to allow Mr. Know-it-all Ranger to find it first. Out of the corner of her eye, she saw it sticking out of a small bush, and she grabbed it before he could get to it. "I've got it!" she called out to him.

As she watched Mr. Ranger, he straightened and sauntered to the hammock. He inspected the knots, probably not trusting that she was capable of tying it properly. Satisfied, he reached out his hand and smiled again from below the dark sunglasses. She wished she could see his whole face.

"Want me to help you get in?"

Roberta backed up.

"I guess not." He frowned. "Well, you watch me, and I'll demonstrate." He backed up to it almost to a sitting position, and then leaned to one side as he sat down. When his back was down, he lifted his legs in. Linking his fingers behind his head and crossing his booted ankles, he appeared quite comfy as the hammock swayed slightly.

"See?" He smiled again.

Roberta glanced up and down his tall frame at the way his lithe body fit into the hammock. He looked tall even lying down, and she guessed his height to be close to six-foot-two. Even though half his face was hidden, he seemed very good-looking. She wondered if he came on like this to all the lone women that came camping.

Roberta grunted in response.

With that infuriating smile still on his face, Mr. Ranger continued to watch her. "This is how you get out." She watched him get out in very much the same manner as he got in.

"Demonstration complete. Have fun." He turned and left, tipping his hat on his way out of the campsite.

Watching him turn down the road and walk away, Roberta sighed. What did he come for this time? If he was going to ask her to pay, he had obviously forgotten all about it when he saw her fall off the hammock. She shuddered to think that he would be back again.

When he was far enough away, Roberta tried once more to enter the hammock, feeling more confident of her ability when he wasn't watching. Doing exactly as Mr. Ranger showed her, she managed to settle in with no more accidents, and sure enough, the hammock was indeed comfy.

Leaning back, she started to read, deciding that maybe camping wasn't such a bad idea after all. As soon as Molly got there, hopefully soon, they could start supper. The only thing she had thought of to bring was hot dogs, and they could build a campfire and roast wieners. She could hardly wait.

The more she read, the more she relaxed, and the more she enjoyed the calming sway of the hammock. Appreciating the lull and the soothing rocking motion, after a couple of chapters, her eyes drifted shut.

≈

The phone rang in the park office.

"Parks and Recreation, Ranger Lamont speaking."

"Garrett? Is that you?" A burst of static blurred the line.

Garrett raised his voice, trying to be heard over all the noise. "Molly? I can't hear you very well. Where are you calling from?"

Molly's voice screamed over the background noise. "I'm calling from the hospital. Mom had another asthma attack. She's going to be fine, but can you go find Robbie? It looks like I won't be there tonight; I have to stay with Mom."

"Your friend never showed up."

Molly gasped. "What do you mean Robbie never showed up? Garrett, she's never pulled a trailer before, and she's got my car and your family's tent trailer. If she's had an accident or something, I'll never forgive myself! It took a while, but I had to really convince her because she's never been camping before. Are you sure she isn't there?"

Garrett's mind raced, trying to fill in the holes obscured by the static. At last, Molly's words sank in. When he had talked to Gwen, he only heard the name Rob, not Robbie, and he naturally assumed it was a guy they were talking about. "Your friend is a she?" Garrett closed his eyes. Robbie. Roberta Garland. The screwy woman in site 27. The hammock that looked just like his. The trailer with the crank that got stuck in the same place. And he had thought the car looked familiar. It was Molly's car.

"Garrett, haven't you met Robbie before?" Molly shouted over the noise. She paused. "But then, she didn't remember ever meeting you either. Maybe you two really haven't met."

Garrett said nothing. No wonder the woman was such a basket case. Gwen had told him earlier that Rob arrived at work to find the fiancé making out with someone else in the storage room. They had an ugly fight in front of all the staff, and after that Rob had promptly been fired. It hadn't dawned on him that Rob could be female. And he had asked her when her boyfriend was coming, he remembered. No wonder she had broken down and cried again.

Garrett knew how persistent Molly could be when she got herself stuck on something, and it appeared she had been at work again, this time convincing her poor dejected friend to go camping to get away from it all. No wonder this Robbie was so incompetent-looking. Not only was it not her tent trailer, she had never even been camping before. Under those circumstances, she hadn't done too badly.

Smiling, he remembered the sight of her sailing over the hammock as it flipped over with her on it. He thought she had seriously hurt herself that time, but instead she had made a joke about losing her book. She had even been friendly, until she remembered to keep her distance from him.

The phone line crackled again.

"Garrett? Are you still there? Hello?"

"Yes, Molly, I'm still here. Just thinking, that's all. And yes, your friend Robbie is here. She's set up and everything is fine. Let's just say she hasn't been too receptive to my assistance." He frowned as he recalled her expression as she screamed at him to leave her alone, then ran sobbing into the camper. "About now she's all settled into my hammock reading a book. Maybe I'd better go introduce myself." The volume of the static increased, and Garrett was ready to end the conversation, but Molly's raised voice again broke through.

"You're going to have to do more than that. I can't come tonight like I promised. I was going to ask if you'd stay with her for the night and keep an eye on her. She's had a pretty rough time of things."

Garrett's frown deepened. Surely Molly was joking. Twice already her friend had screamed at him to leave her alone, and he had no intention of spending a night in the same campsite with a woman, unchaperoned. "I'll talk to her, and see what she says. That's all I'm going to promise, Molly."

"That's fine with me. I have to go; there's someone else waiting for the phone. See you tomorrow after supper when I come with Gwen. What site is she in?"

"Site 27. At least she picked a good spot."

"Great. See you tomorrow, and tell Robbie I'm sorry."

"Sure. Bye, Molly."

Garrett hung up the phone, his ear ringing from both the loud static and Molly's shouting. Now what? Was he going to walk up to this strange woman and say, "Hi, a mutual friend asked me to keep you company"? How about, "Move over, you're in my camper"? Maybe, "Hi, that's my hammock"? An even better line, "Sorry to hear about your fiancé, now I'm here to spend the night with you."

Garrett picked up his hat and sunglasses and put them back on as he walked out the door toward site 27, deep in thought.

❧

Roberta lay in the bottom of a small boat, rocking as the waves sloshed against the side, the lull of the splashing soothing her. Clouds drifted through the bright blue sky. Birds sang overhead.

Suddenly everything darkened. A voice drifted from a cave, and she could feel an evil presence. It called her name. Frightened, she cowered as she continued to lie in the bottom of the boat. A dark claw reached toward her neck, ready to strangle her. A voice called her name, again and again. The ugly clawed hand touched her.

Roberta jolted to a sitting position and screamed. Her arm flung out, still holding the book until it hit something and flew out of her hand with the force of the impact. She swung back and forth, disoriented. Where was she? What was happening?

She gasped for breath as she clung tightly to taut pieces of cloth at her sides. She slowly became aware of her surroundings, to discover herself swinging back and forth in the hammock. Mr. Ranger stood beside her without his hat on, his sunglasses askew on his face, clutching his nose, blood dripping out between his fingers.

Realizing what had happened, Roberta gathered her thoughts, mortified. She had hurt him. She covered her mouth with her hands. "Oh, Mr. Ranger! I'm so sorry!" she gasped. "Mr. Ranger! Are you all right? Let me get something for you!"

Roberta tried to get out of the hammock quickly, but ended up falling out on her hands and knees in her haste. She banged her sore knee for the third time, this time taking off a few layers of skin, causing it to bleed. She tried to ignore it as she ran into the camper for a towel, clutching at her knee, hobbling as fast as she could.

Grateful she had already discovered where the towels were stored, she pulled one out quickly and limped back to Mr. Ranger, offering it to him. "I'm so sorry! I didn't mean to hit you! I feel so awful!"

He removed the sunglasses to press the towel up against his face. "No, no, don't worry about it. I'm sorry for startling you, Robbie. I should have thought before I woke you." He repositioned the towel. "How's your knee? You should get some ice on it." His deep baritone voice came out muffled as he spoke through the towel.

Roberta looked up at him from her crouched position as she continued to press her hand to her wounded knee. This time she could only see the top half of his face. The hat and glasses were gone, but the towel obscured his face from his nose down.

Mr. Ranger had beautiful dark brown eyes, long lashes, and gorgeous thick straight dark hair, wonderfully soft-looking, although it was quite messy from having his hat knocked off. For a brief second she wondered what it would feel like between her fingers.

She shook her head. What was she thinking? She studied the top half of his face, trying to imagine what both halves would look like together.

&

Garrett looked down at Molly's friend as she hunched over clutching her knee. He had sure seen stars when she hit him in the nose with that book. With all the accidents he witnessed today, he should have known better than to get too close.

"What did you call me?" he asked slowly, his voice muffled as he spoke through the towel.

Her face turned red. "I called you Mr. Ranger. For some reason I've been thinking of you as Mr. Ranger in my head every time you've come by. And why did you call me Robbie? Only my friends call me Robbie. How did you know that?"

Garrett shuffled the towel to hold it to his nose with his left hand as Robbie narrowed her eyes to glare daggers at him. He examined his right hand and wiped it on his shorts, just in case, before extending it to her for a handshake.

"Molly just called me. Allow me to introduce myself. I'm Garrett, Gwen's brother. We're going to be camping together."

She stared at him with her mouth open. She did not reach out and shake his extended hand. Instead, all the color drained from her face as she buried her face in her palms.

"Oh, no!" she moaned as she bowed her head.

three

Garrett held the towel away from his face and dabbed at his sore nose with the back of his hand to make sure the bleeding had stopped. In addition to the dull throb on his cheekbone where the frame of his sunglasses had smashed into his face on impact with the book, his eyes still watered from the blow to his nose. If he hadn't been wearing the sunglasses, she would have taken his eye out with the corner of that thing. He had never considered a book to be a lethal weapon before. He'd heard the pen was mightier than the sword, but this was ridiculous.

Garrett looked down at Robbie, who still refused to look at him. She was still hunched over with her face hidden by her hands. With her track record today, Garrett could see why she didn't want to face him, and he felt bad for her, but it couldn't be avoided. They were more or less forced into each other's company. He cleared his throat.

"Molly phoned to say her mother had an asthma attack, and it looks like she's going to stay with her tonight, so she asked me to check up on you. I hope you don't mind."

Robbie uncovered her face and looked up at him with big round green eyes. She didn't say a word.

He ran his fingers through his hair, scrunched his hat in his hand, then stared at the crinkles he made in it. "She also told me what happened. I'm very sorry. I didn't mean to upset you earlier."

When she still didn't say anything, Garrett looked at her again. She remained hunkered down near the ground, looking up at him with big sad doe eyes. Garrett forced himself to smile. This did not look like the start of a fun evening.

He tried to think of something to say, but nothing came to

mind. All he could do was stare down at her. The one time she smiled at him, it struck him how pretty she was. She was pretty even now, almost cowering, her face pale, in that half-kneeling squat. Delicately featured, she had deep sea green eyes and a long flowing wavy mane of beautiful hair, so light brown it was almost blonde.

Earlier, he remembered restraining himself from reaching out and touching her hair to remove the stick that lodged in it after she'd been lying face down on the ground, but he was stopped by her foul expression at the time. At least now he understood why she was in such a state of emotional upheaval.

&

Roberta continued to stare up at Mr. Ranger, better known as Garrett. Molly hadn't mentioned he was a park ranger, but at least now it made more sense why Gwen's brother would be joining them on the camping outing. He worked here.

Without the hat and dark glasses, she could see both halves of his face at the same time. His dark brown hair, so dark it was almost black, suited his strong features. Cut short at the sides and longer on top and at the back, it emphasized his Roman nose, which didn't make him in any way unattractive but instead added to his appeal. The dark tone of his skin matched his deep chocolate brown eyes. They were set off by strong heavy eyebrows that accented the masculine appeal in his face.

A large red blotch marred his right cheek, probably where she had hit him with her book. By tomorrow it would most likely be a big ugly bruise. She tried not to cringe at the knowledge that it was her fault.

If she had to typecast a ranger, he would definitely be a match. Everything about him shouted "the great outdoors." Tall, muscular build. . .he even looked great in shorts, and she hadn't seen many men who had such nice legs. She'd gotten a good view of those legs from the ground up.

All day long she'd made such a fool of herself in front of

him, not to mention how she'd been treating him so badly. Even if she had never liked the know-it-all type, it didn't give her the right to be rude. Not only that, if he was Molly's friend, she would have to be nice to him.

He wiggled the arms of his sunglasses, gently slid them back onto his face, replaced his hat, and smiled, but she didn't smile back. "Let's go sit down somewhere more comfortable." He reached out his hand toward her after wiping it again on his shorts.

She stood on her own, refusing to touch his hand out of rebellion. She agreed to this camping vacation to be left alone, not to have one of the park rangers watch her, even if it was on Molly's request. She knew Molly was only concerned, but she didn't need or want a baby-sitter.

She opened her mouth to protest, but the words died in her throat. The reason for Molly's concern, Mike's betrayal, brought back the image of Mike and Suzie together, and Mike's ugly words as she left the office. She walked to the lawn chairs in silence. She refused to break down and cry. The poor man had seen enough tears. She would be strong. She would get on with her life. Tomorrow.

❧

Garrett ignored being shunned. He watched her limp over to one of the lawn chairs, where she sat all prim and proper, folding her hands in her lap, watching him with those big round sad eyes. He thought what would be best for her would be a good conversation to take her mind off her troubles. "So, how do you like my hammock? I see you had a little nap in it."

"Yes," she replied quietly. "It's very nice." She lowered her head and stared at her hands folded in her lap.

There was a long pause.

"You did a good job setting up the tent trailer, especially for someone who's never been camping before. It even looks level."

"Thank you," she replied equally as quiet. "But you did all the hard parts."

Another long silence.

"You picked a real good campsite. This is one of the largest and most private, with all the trees surrounding it. Quiet too. It will be nice and quiet tonight. Most of the campers who come Thursday just park their units to reserve the spot and leave. It will be full tomorrow night."

"Yes," she nodded, her voice still soft. "That's what Molly said."

More silence.

Garrett resisted dragging his hand over his face. Enough trying to make conversation. He had things to do. He wasn't here on vacation.

"I've got to get back to work now. I'll stop by and peek in on you from time to time. The rangers usually have dinner in about an hour and a half. Since Molly isn't coming, would you care to join us?"

"No, I think I'll stay here. Thanks anyway." She stared down at her lap and picked at a thread.

"By yourself? You don't have to be alone, you know. You're more than welcome to come join us." The other rangers might even be jealous if he brought along a pretty woman to supper break, even if she didn't talk much. Knowing the rest of them, if she remained quiet, they'd all start to show off, trying to impress her. The last laugh would be on them.

"I'll be fine, thank you."

This was one depressed lady. As much as he tried to think of something that would cheer her up, not a thing came to mind. Maybe bringing her into the ranger camp to sit among all the guys wasn't such a great idea, but he did have to agree with Molly: Robbie shouldn't be left alone. He just didn't know what to do about it.

He watched as she sat in the chair, her dainty hands folded in her lap, staring down at them. She was even starting to make him feel depressed. He started to nervously brush a fleck of dirt off his shorts before he stopped himself.

"Look," he said as he stood, "if you don't want to join the rangers for dinner, that's fine. I can come here. I know it's awkward when you don't know anyone. And I'm off around midnight tonight. Maybe we can talk then. I have to go. But I'll see you later, okay, Robbie?"

Roberta finally got enough nerve to meet his eyes. His last statement sounded more like a question, as if he was asking permission to come back. She supposed she couldn't stop him. Roberta reminded herself again that he was Molly's friend.

She raised her head and stared at him. He stared back without speaking.

He adjusted his sunglasses on his face, and touched the brim of his hat. "Well, enjoy yourself. See you at supper time." He turned and strode off, out of the campsite and around the corner.

❧

Garrett walked along the camp road, checking for unregistered arrivals, but he couldn't stop thinking of Robbie. Usually he didn't go for the helpless femme fatale type. He certainly could understand Robbie's downcast spirit, but somehow it didn't add up with her attempt to be a successful camper all by herself or the way she screamed at him earlier, displaying a burst of temper and emotion any five-year-old would have been proud of.

It was probably just as well that she was here rather than at home brooding, except that Molly wouldn't be here until tomorrow night. Although this particular campground was generally family oriented, he didn't like the idea of a woman camping alone. He hadn't exactly been thrilled to hear that Gwen and Molly would be camping by themselves, so he jumped at the chance when Gwen asked him to join them. He had thought he would bow out once Molly's friend Rob arrived, but now it turned out that there would be three women, which wasn't much better. Molly was a bad enough camper, but now Robbie. . .

Until Molly and Gwen arrived, it was up to him to keep an

eye on her, not that he knew what to do or say. Only time would tell.

&

Roberta stared at the empty fire pit. Molly wasn't coming. Bad enough that she let Molly convince her to try this stupid camping idea, but now, except for Mr. Ranger Garrett, she was all alone. She didn't know what to think or what to do.

Not that she cared to admit it, but she was a little nervous all by herself out here, even if her original idea was to be left alone. If Garrett insisted on visiting, that was fine. With any luck, he would get bored and leave soon, having done his duty and fulfilled his promise to Molly. Roberta smiled. Knowing Molly, she could really pour on the pressure. Her own presence in this campground was testimony to that.

Roberta's stomach grumbled. Because of the scene at work and then Molly's arrival at her house, she had skipped lunch. Garrett likely wouldn't leave his good supper and the company of his other park ranger friends to join her for scorched hot dogs, so she was on her own.

She frowned, still staring blankly at the fire pit. She'd had every intention of having a wiener roast with Molly, so she would do her best without Molly. But to have a wiener roast, she first needed a fire. She remembered passing a stockpile of firewood on the way in, so she set on her way to bring a few pieces back to the campsite.

At the entrance to the pullout, she stopped to read a sign about campfire safety, which stated, among other things, that a campfire was not to be left unattended.

She selected a few light dry logs, juggled the load in her arms, trying to ignore the scrape of the rough bark, and wondered how long it would take to burn these few pieces. She paused, studied the large firewood pile again, and decided she would need more, necessitating more than one trip to get enough of a stockpile to last the entire evening. She had nothing better to do anyway, and since the wood was dirty, she thought it best to carry it by hand, rather than get pieces of bark and mud in Molly's clean car.

After the third trip, Roberta lost the bounce to her step. Trudging back and forth in the heat of a summer day, carrying dirty hunks of heavy wood, was not turning out to be her idea of a dream vacation. As she stared at her meager pile of firewood beside her campsite fire pit, she wondered how much more she would need to last the night. It might be hot as anything in the middle of the afternoon, but the evenings cooled quickly, probably more so out here in the wilderness.

She swiped her arm across her forehead and fanned herself by waving the front of her T-shirt. Even though she had been selective, the logs seemed to get heavier with every trip, and she was getting sweaty. She wiggled her foot to dislodge a rock stuck between her toes, not having the energy to remove the sandal and do it properly. She counted the logs in her stash, and decided that one more load ought to do it. How big a fire did it take to cook one lousy wiener, anyway? She wiped her hands on her shorts and headed down the gravel road one last time.

Bent at the waist, picking through the pile for the lightest pieces of a decent size, she heard that all-too-familiar deep baritone voice behind her.

"Hi, Robbie. Want me to carry some for you?"

She cringed, then straightened to look up into those huge dark sunglasses. Even though she couldn't see his eyes, at least now she knew what they looked like.

He stood tall, smiling down at her, his feet slightly apart and his arms crossed over his broad chest. Roberta gulped, then lowered her head to find more nice pieces of wood.

He didn't miss a beat. "I see you're getting a nice little pile of firewood back at the campsite. Between the two of us, one more trip ought to do it."

Back at the campsite? Roberta squeezed her eyes shut. He'd gone looking for her. She wasn't that helpless, or hopeless, that she couldn't do this by herself.

She glared at him in silence. Either he wasn't looking, or he was ignoring her. With those stupid sunglasses, she couldn't get the satisfaction of giving him a dirty look when he wasn't paying attention.

Therefore, she ignored him, continuing to select a few more light dry pieces. Once she selected a good armload, she turned to see him standing beside her, waiting with his arms full, holding approximately triple the amount of wood she did.

She opened her mouth to protest, but self-preservation changed her mind. With the amount of wood he held, she would definitely have enough to last the whole night, plus part of tomorrow, maybe even till Molly and her friend arrived.

"Let's go," she said, instead of the words she really had in mind.

They walked quietly for a few minutes, which was a welcome change. Pleasant voice that he had, he talked far too much for Roberta's liking. Unfortunately, as usual, he was the first to break the silence.

"Don't you just love to sit by a crackling fire in the dark?"

"Uh, sure."

He looked down at her as they walked side by side. "Have you ever made a campfire before?"

Roberta kept her gaze decidedly forward. "No."

"Do you know anything about building a fire?"

"No."

He faced forward again as he continued to talk. "Would you like me to show you? I've got a few free minutes. I can chop up some kindling for you. Since you've got my camper I know where the ax is."

Ax? Kindling? Maybe she could use a little help. If only she had received better instructions from Molly, but since she didn't, she was starting to appreciate Garrett's constant intervention.

She tried to sneak a sideways glance as they walked together. If only Molly hadn't asked him to keep an eye on her, she wouldn't feel like he was only looking after her because he was obligated. But then again, he had helped her quite a bit before he knew who she was.

Roberta decided to be more gracious. "Yes, thank you. I'd appreciate that."

He turned to her, smiling his response. A strange quiver unsettled her stomach, but she convinced herself it was only because she was overhungry. She hated control freaks. Like Mike. Instead of returning his smile, she faced forward and trudged into the campsite.

Garrett opened a compartment on the outside of the trailer and pulled out a rather large ax. Then, to her shock, he started unbuttoning his shirt.

Roberta tried not to gasp. "What are you doing!" she gulped, taking a step backward.

"I thought you wanted me to chop some kindling for you?" he asked as he slung his shirt over the back of one of the lawn chairs. He walked to the pile and selected a couple of larger logs and stood one of them up on end. Holding the ax across the front of him, one hand on the end of the handle and the other about two thirds of the way up, he shuffled his feet to stand with his legs planted firmly apart.

Roberta gulped and stared. Mr. Great Outdoors. Except for the fact that he got on her nerves, Roberta almost wanted to run and get her camera. Standing tall above the log and holding the ax, he looked rugged. Powerful. Broad-shouldered and bare-chested with muscles tensed and ready to swing the heavy ax, he was gorgeous. The hat and dark glasses shielding his face added a touch of mystery to his appearance.

"Stand back," he commanded as he raised his head in her direction to be sure she was a safe distance away.

He lifted the ax high in the air behind his head and swung it solidly, cleanly splitting a thin piece of wood from the log. Repeating the procedure a number of times, he soon reduced the log to a pile of kindling.

Resting the ax on its head, he wiped one arm across his brow, then wiped his hands on his shorts. "I'll split one log more for you, and then I'll be on my way."

All Roberta could do was nod. He pulled off his hat, ran his hands through his hair, then placed the hat back on his head as he scanned the pile for another log to split.

Roberta couldn't help herself. While he sorted through the pile, she ran into the camper to fetch her camera.

Standing in the same pose as before, he held the ax across the front of him and assessed the log. "Where are you? Stand back. And not behind me. If the head of this ax flies off you could get hurt. Always stand to the side of someone chopping wood."

Roberta ran out of the camper around to the side opposite from which he had his head turned, and stood in front of him.

"Robbie? Where are you?"

"Here I am," she called out. As he turned his head to face her, she snapped his picture.

His smile instantly degenerated into a miserable scowl. "What are you doing?" he barked.

"What does it look like I'm doing? I'm going to take your picture. Smile." She deliberately failed to mention that she had already taken one. Raising the camera to her face again, she took a step back. "Come on, smile. Say cheese!"

Garrett did not smile. If looks could kill, Robbie would have been six feet under.

"Put that thing away."

Roberta faced him. Even though she couldn't see his eyes, she could tell from the tight frown that he was more than serious.

He stiffened and let go of the center of the ax handle, holding just the end of it with one hand while the head rested on the ground. "I said put that thing away," he said from between clenched teeth.

She lowered the camera.

"Away. Put it away."

Instead she held it behind her back. "Why don't you like having your picture taken?"

"I just don't. Okay?" His voice was even. Too even. His

teeth were still clenched. Although she obviously didn't know him very well, any fool could see he wasn't kidding. She didn't understand, because up until now, he had been so mild mannered. Roberta decided not to push her luck. She walked back to the camper and placed the camera on the table, while he glowered at her, watching her every step.

Obediently, she stood in an acceptable location while Garrett silently split the other log. Roberta watched in admiration, but said nothing as he repeatedly swung the heavy ax, making perfect, even pieces every time.

When he was done, he remained uncharacteristically silent for possibly the first time. Roberta ran into the camper.

&

Garrett inhaled a deep breath and watched her disappear, still feeling irritable, and hating himself for it. He knew he shouldn't have been so harsh with her; after all, how would she know? The poor woman had enough problems without having to deal with his hang-ups. All he wanted to do was keep an eye on her, and he didn't know why, because she was certainly less than receptive to his presence. He realized he would have kept watching her even if Molly hadn't asked. He rested his hands on his hips and waited, staring toward the camper, wondering what was taking her so long, and if she was going to try anything else with that camera. His gut clenched at the thought of it.

Thankfully, she reappeared, carrying a clean towel, which she handed to him without a word. He lifted his hat and sunglasses with one hand and wiped his face with the towel, then rubbed the sweat off his chest and shoulders. Instead of handing her the damp towel, he threw it over the back of the lawn chair.

"Thanks for the towel," he grumbled as he picked up his shirt, buttoned it, tucked it into the waistband of his shorts, and left before he said something he'd regret.

&

Roberta's stomach grumbled, making her grateful he left

when he did. Before starting the fire to cook her hot dog, she lifted the ax to put it away. As she picked it up, her eye caught the pile of logs. She shifted the weight of the ax in her hands. He had made it look so easy.

Digging through the pile, she found a log that wasn't too big to split. Following Garrett's example, she carefully balanced it up on end, picked up the ax, and touched the blade to the center of the log. She was ready.

The ax was heavier than it looked. She tried lifting it high, but it was too heavy to heave over her head and behind a little bit like Garrett had. Lifting it as high as she could without the fear of falling backwards with it, she swung it down, aiming for the center of the log.

Barely managing to catch it near the edge, the ax buried in a couple of inches and stuck. Roberta pulled and heaved and twisted, trying to free it. In the end, she pushed the log back onto its side, and pushed and wiggled the ax until it came out. She dropped it on the ground, then stopped to catch her breath.

Maybe this woodcutting business was best left alone.

With very little effort, she soon had a good fire roaring, and her hot dog was nicely roasted. She prepared her supper, then stared at the plate in her lap. It had been so long since she stopped to be thankful for God's blessings, yet today, surrounded by the beauty of God's creation, she felt compelled to offer a prayer of thanks, as she sat in the wilderness, alone.

And she could be thankful. Molly was with her mother, who was fine after her asthma attack. Despite losing her job, she would be fine financially with the severance package. She wouldn't starve or anything; she knew lots of places in the outer areas of Vancouver to apply for another job. And somewhere in Vancouver, Mike and Suzie were having a great time now that she was gone.

Mike. Her teeth clenched. It wasn't God's fault Mike was an unfaithful jerk. She really should have known what kind of guy he was. At first, Mike said he "kind of" believed in God, and he even had attended church a few times with her. Soon, he convinced her to start missing services, until she hadn't been going for months. She wondered if Mike was ever a believer, and she suspected he had gone to church with her in the beginning only to win her trust. What a sucker she had been. He was no loss. Now that the shock was over, she was thankful she found out in time. The only loss was her job.

And so what? There were lots of other jobs out there. Her best friend, Molly, had come to her rescue, providing a break from routine in which to get her head together. Garrett, Molly's friend's brother, was there to help her, should she need it, even though he got on her nerves.

Roberta bowed her head and thanked God for taking care of all her needs. Just as she raised her head and lifted the hot dog to her mouth, a familiar voice echoed behind her.

"Nice fire. Looks like you're going to make a decent camper yet. And I see you found the roasting poles. Am I invited?"

Roberta turned around to see Garrett's lithe form striding to the fire pit, all traces of his anger from their last encounter forgotten. She had been enjoying the silence until now.

"Help yourself. Everything I brought is in the cooler." She doubted what she brought for Molly would be enough for a big man like him, but what she had, he was welcome to share.

She heard him digging through the cooler, pausing every once in a while to open a few lids.

"Hey, potato salad, great! And carrots, already cut up and everything. And this looks like grape juice. You sure I can help myself?"

"That's what I said."

Roberta heard him without really paying attention to what he was saying as he complimented her on the food she brought, comparing it to an allegedly miserable campfire meal at the ranger camp. He stepped into the camper to get himself a plate and utensils, yakking constantly the entire time. She hoped he would at least be quiet while he was eating.

Plate full, he sauntered to the campfire, dragging a lawn

chair with him. He smiled as he accepted the pole with his hot dog. She ate her dinner, nodding politely as he kept up enough conversation for both of them, until finished roasting his supper.

Conversation abruptly stopped. Just in case he was choking on his dinner, Roberta turned her head to check on him. Garrett sat in the lawn chair, his head bowed. She stared as he didn't move or speak for a few seconds. He nodded once, still silent, then raised his head. Even though she couldn't see his eyes through the sunglasses, she knew he was staring back at her.

"Yes?" he asked, then opened his mouth and took a massive bite out of his hot dog.

four

Roberta concentrated intently on the fire, poking the glowing embers with a long stick she had found earlier.

He prayed over his meal. Discreetly. Without any prompting.

She didn't know anything about him, nor did she know what Molly had told him about her. Did he know about her situation with Mike? After Mike making all the right moves to earn her trust, she wasn't so sure that Garrett wouldn't do the same. Pretending to be a committed Christian had done wonders for Mike. She wouldn't fall for that again.

"I like this brand of potato salad. I buy this kind, too."

She'd have to ask Molly more about him, just to satisfy her curiosity. Until then, she planned to keep her distance.

"Did you bring any marshmallows? If not, I can bring a bag from our stash at ranger headquarters." His sly little grin told her there was more to the story, but she didn't ask for more details.

She shook her head.

He checked his watch. "Time for me to get back. I'll check in on you when I make the rounds. Catch you later, and thanks for supper, Robbie. I always love a home-cooked meal."

Home-cooked meal? Flame-blackened hot dogs and store-bought potato salad? She did cut the carrots by hand, though. "You're welcome."

Standing at the same time, she turned and watched him leave the campsite. Instead of walking, he drove away in a small pickup truck with the Parks and Recreation logo painted on the door.

She carefully settled into the hammock with her book after she washed the dishes, which took a considerable amount of time since she had to heat the water first. She only managed to read part of a chapter, when she started to experience difficulty reading. Daylight had faded considerably, and tucked inside the hammock, it was even darker. She knew how black the night became when there was a power failure, and she suspected that here in the middle of nowhere, without the far-off glow of any city lights, it would be even blacker. She remembered coming across a lantern, and she decided to light it before it got too dark to make out the instructions.

Although she thought she turned all the knobs and things to the right place, she wasn't positively sure she did everything exactly right. Of course, this was the only time she wished Mr. Know-it-all Ranger Garrett were here, and just her luck, he was nowhere to be seen. As a precaution, she carried the camper's fire extinguisher outside.

Before attempting to light the lantern, she walked to the entrance of the campsite and looked both ways down the road for Garrett. Naturally, since she was actually hoping to see him, she didn't.

In the few minutes it took her to check down the road, the sky continued to darken, reminding her that she couldn't wait forever. Earlier she recalled yelling at him that she didn't care if she blew herself up. This was her chance to prove it.

Taking a deep breath for courage, she studied the lantern, the lighter in one hand and the fire extinguisher at her feet. Using her flashlight, to be on the safe side she tilted her head and ran her finger down the worn instructions on the lantern to read them once more. She pumped it till her best guess thought it was right, flicked the lighter on, and held the flame in the little hole with the arrow on it.

A poof sounded as it caught, but no explosion ensued. However a small flame burned on the outside casing where she had dribbled some fuel, and the thing sputtered and hissed and flickered ominously. Hoping for the best but expecting the worst, she pulled the pin, aimed the fire extinguisher, and waited.

"Let me guess. You've never worked a lantern before."

The sudden deep timbre of that voice nearly made her pull the trigger. If the thing hadn't blown up yet, she was probably safe. She lowered the fire extinguisher to her side and glared at Garrett. "What gave me away? My shaking knees or the fire extinguisher?"

Garrett laughed so hard he had to wipe tears from his eyes, which made Roberta notice he wasn't wearing the sunglasses any more. Of course, it was dark so he didn't need them, but by now she was beginning to wonder if he slept with them on. He had also changed out of his shorts, and now wore uniform pants; the stripes on the side emphasized the length of his legs.

He laughed as he spoke. "Sorry for laughing. The fire extinguisher was actually a good idea, especially with your track record today." He paused and wiped his eyes again. "More people should do that. I've seen a couple of those things catch fire. Congratulations. You've got more sense than some of the jokers that come here."

Roberta wasn't sure if she should take that as a compliment or not.

He continued to laugh. "In fact, I could tell you stories about what people set on fire out here."

She wasn't amused. She didn't want to hear about it, but she knew that by the end of her camping vacation, she proba-bly would anyway.

During the course of his laughter, the flame on the outside of the lantern burned itself out. "Here. Let me set it for you." He pumped it up a bit more to brighten it, and adjusted one of the knobs. The annoying hissing faded to an acceptable level. "There. How's that?"

While bright enough to cast some questionable shadows among the trees, the light seemed to waver, making it difficult to imagine doing much with it. "Is that as bright as it gets? What am I supposed to do in this? It's still dark."

"It's not exactly a quartz-halogen spotlight. This is a camp-site, not an art studio. Most people only sit around the campfire and roast marshmallows and stuff. If you sit close enough, you may be able to read your book if it isn't too small a print. But if you get near that book again, I'm afraid I'm going to have to keep my distance."

"Really? Promise?"

Garrett almost looked hurt, but then he smiled, probably thinking she was joking. "No," he replied.

It was just as well for the moment. She needed a favor. "I have to make a trip to the outhouse. Can you stand here and watch the fire for me? The sign said not to leave a fire unattended, and since you're one of the park authorities, I figure you'd be a good one to ask."

"I'd be honored," he said solemnly. Garrett removed his hat and held it over his heart and bowed.

"Very funny," Roberta grumbled. "I'll be right back." She made a hasty retreat to the ladies' outhouse, which was a few sites down the road. Away from the fire, the air possessed a chill, convincing her to change into her jeans when she got back to the camper.

On her way out of the facilities, a man stood at the side, nearly scaring the life out of her.

"Hi there," he said. He quite obviously scanned her from head to foot, then smiled.

She would have stepped back into the outhouse, except she didn't want to appear frightened. Roberta looked around, hoping he was talking to someone else. No such luck. The sunset had nearly faded, making her wish she had brought her flashlight, if not for the light, for a weapon. "Are you talking to me?" she asked, checking around one more time.

"Yes. I've been watching you. Are you alone?"

The hairs on the back of her neck rose in alarm. "Me? Alone? Of course not."

He stepped closer. "Don't be frightened. I'll keep you company."

Her heart stopped, then picked up in double-time. If he knew she was alone and he only wanted someone to talk to, he could have approached her during the daylight in the wide open spaces, not in the bush at dusk when there was no one else around.

Throwing dignity to the wind in favor of personal safety, Roberta stepped sideways, heading for the path to the open gravel road. She forced herself to speak louder than usual, trying her best to keep the tremor out of her voice as she backed up. "I'm not interested in any company. Come any closer, and I'll scream!" Not giving him a chance to respond, she ran back to her campsite, where Garrett stood beside the campfire, his arms crossed over his chest.

"You took an awful long time. I was getting ready to come and get you." He paused as he glanced up and down her. "Are you all right? You seem a little out of breath."

If she told him about the stranger who approached her, he'd never leave her alone. She shook her head, then stared at the entranceway to the campsite to make sure she hadn't been followed. "I'm fine, thank you," she gulped.

Garrett frowned. "I'm off duty after we close the park gate at 11:00. I'll be back after midnight, after everything is settled, if you're still up by then."

Roberta tried very hard not to check her watch to see how much longer that would be. Like a fool, she had run straight back to her own campsite for the strange man to plainly see where she was staying. If he didn't already know which site was hers, he knew now. For the first time today, she didn't want to be left alone. She contemplated locking herself in the car until Garrett came back. Or maybe she should just leave. If she left the camper as it was, all set up, it would take her less than an hour to get back home where she would be safe.

But she wasn't going to let some stranger manipulate her. All her life, she'd allowed people to lead her and manipulate her for their own gain. Roberta steeled her nerve. That was about to stop. The stranger was probably harmless. Besides, if she got into any kind of trouble, any scream in the relative quiet of the campground would be heard for miles, and someone would come quickly to her assistance. She smiled at Garrett. "Sure. I'd like that very much. See you then."

Roberta expected him to nod and leave, but he didn't. He narrowed his eyes and held eye contact, as if studying her. He turned his head to the road, then back to her. She suspected she had taken too long to reply, or been a little too eager for his return, because he was looking at her funny. Up until now, he always smiled and left quickly, but this time he didn't.

"I'll be right back," he said curtly, walked to the road, hopped into the park truck, and drove away.

Roberta sat beside the fire. To try to calm her nerves, she concentrated on the noises of the night. Frogs croaked and crickets chirped in the distance. She couldn't hear any birds or squirrels like during the day. Every once in a while she heard what must be a coyote far in the background.

And the stars. Without the city lights, double or triple the number of stars was visible, twinkling in the black night sky. It was beautiful and peaceful.

And cold.

Even though she changed into her jeans, she still shivered. Flashlight in hand, she fetched her jacket from the camper. Before she stepped out, she peeked to be sure no one had come into the campsite when she wasn't looking.

She chided herself for being so paranoid. She returned to the lawn chair beside the fire and continued to look up at the sky. Molly was right. Sitting beneath God's heavens was a great way to unwind.

She had no idea how much time had passed when she again heard footsteps. Despite the speech she gave to herself to calm her jitters, she squealed and jumped out of the chair, turning to face the intruder.

"Hi there. Miss me?"

Her breath released in a whoosh. It was only Garrett. This time she didn't dread his arrival.

"Oh. Hi. Have a seat. After all, they're your lawn chairs." She smiled at him.

Instead of joining her at the fire, he walked to the camper and threw in a duffel bag that had been slung over his shoulder.

"What was that?"

"Just my stuff."

"Stuff?" Roberta narrowed her eyes and stared at him. "What kind of stuff?"

"Just my toothbrush and sleeping bag and stuff. After all, I'm going to need it."

"Need it?"

"Molly asked me to keep an eye on you, and I don't feel comfortable about a woman spending the night all alone out here."

"You're not serious," she demanded more than she asked.

"Yes, I am," he stated, very seriously.

"No, you're not."

"Yes, I am. It's my camper."

Roberta tapped her foot and crossed her arms. "Now, hold on."

Garrett repressed a smile, then imitated her position, crossing his arms in response. He towered above her, but Roberta refused to be intimidated.

"Listen. Something frightened you earlier, even though you wouldn't admit it."

She couldn't deny it, so instead, she gave him her best menacing look.

This time he noticed. He grinned. "Molly told me to look after you. You don't want to cross Molly, do you?"

She opened her mouth to tell him she didn't care what Molly thought or did, but he interrupted her.

"This is no big deal, you know. When I'm not working here, I live with my mother and my sister. I can respect your privacy if you can respect mine."

"No way. It's not proper." It didn't matter that he was Molly's friend's brother. She didn't know him. Even if she did, she wasn't sharing accommodation with a man.

"It's a camper, a combination living room, kitchen, and

everything else rolled into one. You get one side, I get the other. It's okay."

"No way."

"Fine. Then I'll sleep in my pup tent, but I'm staying in this campsite tonight."

Her mouth opened, then snapped shut. Up until that strange man approached her near the outhouse, she had been nervous, but she had been perfectly willing to spend the night alone. Now she wasn't so sure. If Garrett, an official park ranger, and a big one at that, stayed in the campsite, she would be safe. Her only alternative was to go home, and that would be admitting defeat. He could stay. In his pup tent.

"All right, but you'd better not snore or walk in your sleep or anything bizarre."

He placed one hand over his heart and lifted up the other arm elbow height in the form of a pledge. "Not me. Scout's honor."

Roberta crossed her arms and tilted her head to one side. "Have you ever been a scout?"

He grinned. "No. But I'm the park ranger. Does that count?"

"Maybe," she grumbled. If he had said anything about being a born-again Christian as evidence of his virtue, she would have screamed and left.

"Good." He dropped his hands to his sides. He threw a few more logs on the fire, and both of them sat on the lawn chairs in front of the fire. Following his example, Roberta leaned forward to warm her hands above the fire.

"I thought you were working until after midnight."

"I booked off. Someone's covering for me. They know where I am if they need me."

"Oh."

The fire snapped and crackled as it burned. Sparks flew upward into the night, illuminating the surrounding area, until they darkened and floated to the ground as ash. The lantern, hissing slightly on the table, only illuminated the immediate area. In the blackness, the night seemed more still and peaceful than the most deserted city street.

Garrett's voice seemed unnaturally loud in the pristine night. "Want to talk?"

She knew the golden silence couldn't last. "About what?"

Bent over in the chair with his palms raised to the fire and elbows on his knees, he shrugged his shoulders. "Oh, anything. The weather. Cars. Your love life."

Her love life.

Frogs croaked somewhere in the background. Probably Momma frogs and baby frogs. She'd never have baby frogs. "I don't have a love life. Not anymore."

"I heard."

Part of the problem was that she didn't know what Molly had told him. Roberta sighed. "What did you hear?"

Thankfully, he continued to look into the fire. She couldn't have faced anyone right then. "Molly told Gwen who told me that you caught your fiancé cheating on you, you had a fight and he dumped you, and then you got fired. That's all I know."

"Something like that." Roberta snorted. The more she thought about it, the stupider she felt. How could she not have seen it coming? "You don't want details, do you?"

"Only if you want to tell me. I'm a pretty good listener."

So she told him. She didn't know why, but she told him. She hadn't even told Molly, her best friend, all her deepest inner thoughts. Her concentration didn't leave the fire as the whole story poured out. She told him how Mike was the boss's son, about how after years of working there how flattered she'd been when he started paying attention to her. She'd been so excited when Mike started to attend church with her, doing and saying all the right things, claiming to share her beliefs and faith in God. How when Mike talked of family, children, and then marriage she'd been thrilled. She didn't want to be a society wife, but when the time came for Mike to take over his father's company, as his wife, she would have had a social position to uphold and maintain, and she would have accepted that and done her duty. She was happy; she would have done anything for him.

Soon after their engagement became official, Mike started missing church. At first she went alone, but soon he convinced her to start skipping services. The time came when she discovered she hadn't been to church for months. All the while, Mike kept pressing her to sleep with him. She refused.

Then she started picking up on little rumors. With her head in the clouds, she ignored them, which led to this morning, catching him with another woman, in a compromising position. She even told Garrett of her humiliation when they argued in the women's washroom, screaming for everyone in the office to hear. Following that, she was fired. Now here she was, staring blankly into a fire in the middle of nowhere, pouring her heart out to a stranger.

And after it was all out, her eyes remained dry. Saying it out loud rather than brooding about it put everything into a new perspective. Thinking back to the past few months, if she were as in love with Mike as she should have been, wouldn't she be more upset talking about it? When had the relationship started to deteriorate? The more she thought about it, the more she began to wonder. She had been so caught up in the flurry of their engagement, pending plans, discussions of the future, meeting his friends, family, and business acquaintances, she hadn't realized the state of their declining relationship. How had she allowed Mike to sweep her off her feet? From now on, she would not be charmed, romanced, or otherwise participate in any flirtations unless she made the first move.

She continued to stare into the fire, warming her hands. Her backside was getting cold, but she ignored the discomfort as she continued to think. Despite the trauma and hardship of losing her job, maybe this wasn't such a bad thing.

∂⋆

Garrett didn't say a word. He didn't think he needed to. Robbie sat beside him, lost in thought. After her sad story, he was surprised she wasn't crying like she had been earlier today, but that was a good sign. Since he didn't want to ruin a good thing, he continued to sit with his hands raised to the fire, waiting for her to make the first move. He'd promised to be a good listener, so he would listen. If she wasn't talking, he'd listen anyway.

For the life of him, he couldn't understand why she poured her heart out to him. Once she got started, she just didn't stop, unlike her guarded silence until this point. All day long, whenever he checked up on her, he had the distinct impression she couldn't wait to get rid of him. Of course screaming at him to leave her alone while she sobbed her guts out and ran into the camper was a dead giveaway. Although it hurt his ego just a little, he could understand her reaction, especially after hearing about how this Mike guy had treated her.

Robbie could use a friend, and since Molly wasn't there, the duty befell him. Funny thing, he didn't mind. He looked forward to spending the next day alone with her, in between his ranger duties.

Robbie yawned, and Garrett noticed she made no attempt to stifle it. She stood, so he did the same. "I'm really tired," she said. "I've had a rough day and I think I'm going to turn in. You can stay up if you want."

Garrett shook his head. "No, us rangers have to be up and on duty by sunrise. I think I'm going to hit the sack, too."

He stood side by side with Robbie, then turned to face her. Standing nearly toe to toe, he looked down at her. He hadn't realized she was so short. In all their many interactions today, either they'd never both stood at the same time, or if they had, they'd been too far apart to judge the height difference. She must be nearly a foot shorter than he was.

The flickering firelight in the black night made her eyes luminous. All he could do was look down at her as those beautiful eyes widened. She raised both her hands to her mouth. "Oh, Garrett, your face!"

He blinked a couple of times, but he couldn't figure what she meant.

Before he had time to think, one of her tiny hands raised

until her fingertips gently brushed his cheek. He didn't move. He kind of liked it.

"A bruise. And it's all my fault. I'm so sorry."

He covered her hand with one of his, pressing it into his cheek. "Don't worry about it. It doesn't hurt."

She made no attempt to pull away. He didn't know why he did it, but Garrett rested his hands on her shoulders and massaged the back of her neck with his thumbs. "You feeling better?"

She smiled as her hand dropped to her side. "Yes, I am. Thank you."

Instead of the friendly gesture he meant it to be, he wrapped his arms around her and gently pulled her in for a hug. At first she stiffened, but then she relaxed and leaned into him, tucked in neatly underneath his chin. Her whole body from head to toe leaned against him, making his pulse heat up and his brain freeze. They'd only just met that afternoon, but it felt right to hold her in silence. And it scared him.

He'd had a few relationships with women, but never anything serious. At twenty-six years old, he'd begun to wonder if any woman would ignite that spark. Not that he'd given up on finding that special woman, but he'd spent many hours in prayer, turning it over to God. If the woman who was to be his soul mate was out there, God would allow her to cross his path, or he would remain single.

Not that Robbie was his type, but holding her felt comfortable. Perhaps he was going to be the friend she needed to help her recover from the unpleasant situation she found herself in. And he thanked God for the opportunity.

Before he did or said something stupid, he released her. "I'm going to set up the tent. Then I'll douse the fire and turn off the lantern."

Roberta held back a shiver when Garrett released her. No one had ever held her like that. Her parents had nicely patted her on the head when she needed comforting, Mike only held her when he had more than a friendly hug in mind, and she never touched her female friends. When he smiled and backed up, then disappeared into the camper, she felt the loss.

While he was gone, Roberta sat back down in her lawn chair and warmed her hands at the fire. He came back out wearing a T-shirt and sweatpants, with an unzipped jacket. He held the tent poles in his arms. "Now I know why you didn't have the tent to go with these. I had it."

Roberta mumbled good night as she stepped into the camper. Copying Garrett, she also changed into an old T-shirt and her sweatpants to sleep in. And she kept her socks on. Making sure her flashlight was within arm's reach, she pulled the sleeping bag up to her chin.

She unzipped the window to watch Garrett quench the fire. He poked it a few times to be sure it was completely out, then turned off the lantern. Rather than let him trip in the pitch black night, Roberta shone the flashlight through the screened window to allow him to make his way to the tent, but he pulled a solid heavy-duty flashlight with the Parks and Recreation logo on it out of his pocket. "Thanks for the thought, but I came prepared." He grinned and turned the flashlight on to guide his way to the tent door.

Feeling like an idiot, Roberta turned hers off and zipped the window shut.

She listened in the dark to the sound of the zipper on Garrett's sleeping bag.

"Good night, Robbie," he called. "Sleep tight."

Easy for him to say. "Good night, Garrett."

Roberta tucked her flashlight where she could reach it if need be and closed her eyes. Soon the sleeping bag warmed up inside, surrounding her like a warm cocoon. She started to doze off, until crunching sounded in the gravel outside, like someone walking. Her heart pounded, and her eyes jolted open wide, but she saw only blackness. She swallowed hard to make her voice work.

"Garrett!" she forced out. "Garrett! Are you sleeping? Do you hear something? Garrett!"

&

Garrett was already awake. He heard something, or rather, someone, prowling around. If it was one of the other rangers needing something, they would have called him on his radio first. To his knowledge, the camp never had any trouble with intruders, but there was always a first time. This was definitely not an animal, at least not the four-legged kind.

He tried to make his voice sound sleepy and unconcerned, when deep down he was furious. Had someone bothered her earlier, when she was alone?

"Go back to sleep, darling, it's probably just a raccoon," he said loudly enough for anyone to hear a male voice plainly. He hoped the intruder would fail to notice the tent in the darkness and would think his voice came from inside the camper.

The gravel crunched, getting softer, then fading to nothing.

"It's gone. Go back to sleep, Robbie."

&

Roberta could do nothing of the kind. Darling? Who was he calling darling? Certainly not her. He sounded half asleep, so maybe in his dreams he was thinking of a girlfriend. She hadn't thought about it before, and it hadn't occurred to her that he had a girlfriend, but why not? Just because she didn't like him didn't mean no one else could. Whoever "darling" was, the poor woman would have a hard time competing for airtime.

Still, she didn't think it was a raccoon, but Garrett was the park ranger, so if he thought it sounded like a raccoon, it must have been a raccoon. But thoughts of wild animals were the least of her concerns. Now that she was fully awake, she had to go to the outhouse. Tomorrow night, and every night while she was out camping, she would remember to limit her liquid intake.

&

Garrett lay awake, thinking. How was he going to alert the other rangers to be on the lookout for a prowler? He had his walkie-talkie, but in the small space of the campsite, she would hear every word he said, and he didn't want that. How could he sneak off to contact the other rangers?

"Garrett? Are you sleeping?"

Sleeping? Who was she kidding? He was lying there plotting how he could sneak off. "No, I'm not sleeping. What's on your mind?" Hopefully she wasn't scared, even though this time she had a reason to be.

"Garrett, I have to make a trip to the outhouse."

Great! This was his chance. He unzipped the tent and turned on his flashlight, then slipped his feet into his untied hiking boots. Robbie's head stuck out from the camper door. Trying to control his anticipation, he stretched his arms over his head and lowered his voice, trying to look bored. "Mmm. Okay, let's go." Not taking the time to tie the laces, he shone the flashlight on the camper's single stair so she wouldn't trip. As she closed the door behind her, he patted his walkie-talkie in his back pocket.

They walked in silence to the outhouses, where he waited for her on the path. When she was inside, he called the office and told them about someone possibly trespassing in site 27 and asked them to be on the lookout for someone checking out the campsites while people were asleep. He almost wished it was his turn for night duty.

"Who are you talking to?"

Garrett tried not to flinch at the sound of her voice. He hadn't heard her come out of the outhouse. Someone must have finally oiled the hinge. Of all the timing.

"Oh, just checking up on the other rangers, that's all." He held out the walkie-talkie for her to see and turned it off. "Let's get back to sleep, shall we?"

They walked back to the camper in silence. Garrett shone the light for her as she crawled back into the camper, and listened as she zipped up her sleeping bag, then turned off the light and crawled into the tent.

"Good night, Garrett, and thank you," she called softly.

"Good night, Robbie, and you're welcome." Why had he called her "darling"?

five

Daylight came early in the wilderness. Roberta awoke to the smell of coffee and the sound of faint stirrings outside. She opened her eyes, orienting herself to the small sleeping compartment of Garrett's camper. The early light gave the unit a strange glow, giving everything inside a yellowish hue. As soon as she opened the camper door, she smelled food. Good food. Bacon and eggs. Garrett stood beside the picnic table, with a small green camper's cookstove.

Trying to be discreet, she quietly slipped out of the camper and up the entrance to the campsite for a trip to the outhouse. She almost thought she made it undetected, but his head turned, and he smiled and nodded as she left.

Upon her return, two plates of bacon and eggs and toast, and two cups of steaming coffee sat on the picnic table.

"Good morning, Robbie. Did you sleep well? I did."

"How did you cook this out here? Are we going to eat all this for breakfast? What time is it?"

He turned off the flame and raised his head to the sunrise, the brilliant colors already starting to fade. "5:17 A.M."

Roberta looked up. Wisps of pink and purple clouds were losing their colors to bright white against the blue of the early morning sky as she watched. Birds twittered and squirrels chattered. "How could you tell that?"

"I checked my watch."

She would have said something nasty if her stomach hadn't growled. "Where did you get that thing?" She swooshed her hand in the air over the stove. "And all this food?"

"Ranger camp. I've got connections. I make breakfast like this every day."

"If I ate breakfast like this every day I'd weigh six hundred pounds. I brought cereal for breakfast. And I've got milk in the cooler that's got to be used up."

"I suppose we could eat that too. Unless it's some kind of healthy granola stuff. I won't eat that."

She had always assumed that anyone who made a career out of being in touch with nature would lead a healthy lifestyle, including plenty of exercise as well as a nutritionally balanced diet. Somehow, she couldn't see a breakfast of high-fat, high-cholesterol bacon and eggs with thickly buttered toast fitting into that plan.

"It's sugar-sweetened processed kid's cereal, loaded with food coloring and preservatives. Multicolored sugar bombs. The kind my mother would never allow me to have when I was a kid. You're welcome to help yourself if you want."

He grinned ear to ear and rubbed his tummy, which she couldn't help but notice was extremely flat. "Yummy."

A plastic tablecloth covered the picnic table. Despite the questionable nutritional value, not to mention the megacaloric content of the food, she could hardly wait to dig in. This time, she knew what to expect as he sat down. Just as he started to close his eyes, she stopped him. "It's okay, Garrett, you can pray out loud."

His eyes widened as his head rose. He stared blankly at her, then smiled again. Something inside her stomach flipped, but she was sure it was only the growlies.

He bowed his head and folded his hands on the table. "Thank You, dear Lord, for all You've given us, including this food, this wonderful day, and that we can share it with our friends. Amen."

At Roberta's mumbled amen, he dug in. Not only did he consume a huge plate of his own breakfast, but he also helped himself to a large bowl of cereal. He even drank every last drop of the milk.

He turned his wrist to read his watch as he chewed his last mouthful. "Sorry to be rude. I'm on duty, and I'm late."

While she stared at his empty plate and her still half-full

one, Garrett disappeared into the camper. In what seemed like seconds, he reappeared in his uniform, including the pants with the stripe down the side, the hat, and the dark sunglasses to complete the picture. He'd also done up the laces on his hiking boots. She wondered what the outfit would look like with a tie. From the dark shadow on his jaw, she suspected he would be shaving at the ranger camp, where they probably had electricity.

"I've got beach duty after lunch. Want to go for a swim?"

"Swim?"

"There's a beach down that path over there. It takes about fifteen minutes to walk. You can swim, can't you?"

"Of course I can swim!"

"Good. See you after lunch." Tipping his hat, he smiled beneath the sunglasses and walked away with his duffel bag slung over his shoulder and his rolled-up pup tent under his arm, and Roberta couldn't help but notice that he'd again forgotten the poles to go with it.

Roberta dragged her hand over her face. She had been railroaded again. Yesterday Molly had wangled her into going on this camping vacation, and now Mr. Ranger Garrett had conned her into a swimming expedition. Plus, he left her to do all the dirty dishes.

Since it was so early, despite all the time it took to heat the water on the propane elements and repack all the dishes in their plastic boxes once they were clean and dry, she had plenty of time before lunch and Garrett's expected return. Unless he made the rounds as often as he did yesterday.

Short of hiding, she considered what she could do and where she could go that he wouldn't find her. Very few people were in the campground, and those that were, she suspected, were mostly still asleep. The only place she'd seen so far besides her own campsite was the wood stockpile at the entrance. She had seen a sign directing campers to a nature trail, so she decided to check it out.

Preparing for the heat of the day, she changed into her shorts and sandals. After brushing her teeth, she picked up her camera and the rest of the bag of bread that Garrett brought, and she was on her way. If she had three hours to kill, she might as well feed the squirrels or any other wildlife that came along.

After constantly stabbing her toes on twigs and mulch as she walked, Roberta settled down on a log and spent most of her time trying to take pictures of a very elusive squirrel who must have felt the same way as Garrett about having its picture taken. For a while, every time she clicked the camera or moved slightly, the squirrel ran away, but after a few tries, he seemed to get used to her and finally ate in front of her. She wondered how one tiny squirrel could eat so much at once, and why he sometimes hid while he was eating it. However, she still managed to get a few good shots of the squirrel with a tiny piece of bread tucked neatly between its cute little front paws.

The little critter must have sent out some kind of secret squirrel radar code, because just as she was about to leave, a whole flock of squirrels descended from the trees, and before she knew it, the whole loaf was gone, except for two pieces she remembered at the last minute to save for her own lunch. She wondered if other campers gave the squirrels the good pieces, and left the crusts for themselves. Once they saw no more food forthcoming, the squirrels deserted her, so she braved the path again, constantly stopping to empty pieces of the great outdoors from her sandals. Next time, she would wear sneakers.

With no sign of Garrett when she arrived at the campsite, she made herself a sandwich and enjoyed her lunch in peace.

"So there you are. I've been looking for you. Where were you?"

"I went for a walk to feed the squirrels."

Sunlight glinted off his sunglasses as he crossed his arms over his chest, and tilted his shoulders slightly back, presenting an intimidating stance, if she hadn't remembered how tender his embrace could be. "I didn't know where you were.

You were gone a long time."

"So?"

His frown deepened. "I was worried."

"I wanted to be alone and check out Mother Nature, okay? You've been very nice to step in when I needed help and keep an eye on me, but you don't have to check up on me every minute of every day."

Garrett lifted his hat, swiped his hair back, then replaced his hat. "Maybe I have been overdoing it a bit. I apologize."

All the harsh words she nearly let loose were forgotten at the sight of his smile. For such an annoying man, he really had a kind smile.

"I'm sorry, too. I didn't mean to snap at you. You've been very kind, and I do appreciate it. I guess I haven't been myself lately."

"I can understand that. Still want to go to the beach?"

She opened her mouth to protest, but the words didn't come out. It wasn't as if she had anything better to do. She nodded. "Sure. It'll only take me a minute to change."

They walked to the beach in silence at first, but soon Garrett started explaining things he probably thought might interest her along their way, pointing things out in the strangest places. Roberta said very little, content to listen. Some of the things he said were interesting.

Garrett couldn't help himself. Towering above her as they walked side by side, he tried to be a gentleman and not gawk at Robbie in her bathing suit. Most women would have draped their towels over their shoulders as they walked. Just his luck, she wasn't most women. She wrapped the towel around her waist like a skirt, and instead of her dainty little sandals, she wore a tiny pair of pristine white sneakers and little white ankle socks with baby pink pompoms on the back. They wouldn't stay that way for long. He felt like Grizzly Adams clomping along beside her in his favorite hiking boots.

Instead of staring, all he could do was look around and talk about points of interest along the way. He also talked about things that weren't very interesting. Anything. Plants. Animals. Birds. He wasn't usually such a motormouth, but he had to do something, anything rather than stare.

He turned his head as he pointed and explained about a particular species of squirrel that chattered at them in the treetops. He made the mistake of glancing at her when she asked a question. Garrett squeezed his eyes shut for a second and pointedly kept his focus straight ahead from that point on.

The near-deserted beach stretched out before them. Garrett assured her that tomorrow would be another story. In a few hours, people would start arriving as they got off work for the weekend.

"Enjoy it while you can." He sat on the grass and leaned back, resting his weight on his palms, his arms stretched out straight a little behind him, his ankles crossed.

"Aren't you coming in?"

"Nope. I'm on duty." For a second, he almost hoped the expression on her face was one of disappointment, but she simply shrugged her shoulders, untied the towel from her waist, then laid it out on the ground. She ran into the water, then at the right depth, lifted her arms over her head and dove in the rest of the way.

Robbie shot up out of the water, glistening in the sunlight as a spray of water splashed around her. She arched her back, tipped her head backward, and used both hands to swipe her wet hair from her face, then stretched her hands to the sky, radiating total freedom.

He forced himself to blink and added up the hours until he was off duty.

She smiled and waved and dove back in. Garrett forced himself to start breathing again. The next time she came up, she started walking toward the shore, so he stood and walked to the water's edge to meet her. "This is wonderful!" she called from the waist-deep water.

Rather than stand there staring like an idiot, Garrett turned his head and noticed a movement in the designated picnic section. He raised his hands to his mouth to call out to her. "There's someone with a dog in the restricted area. I've got to go kick them off. I'll be right back."

Roberta waved as he walked away, then turned around to dive into the cool water once again. She'd never been swimming alone, but with Garrett on the shore, she didn't feel alone, until he left. She swam back and forth a few times, then stood still to catch her breath.

As she stood, she heard a child splashing nearby and turned to watch. A little boy about four years old played happily on a float toy in water that was almost shoulder height on herself, but there was no adult beside him. Worried, she glanced around the near vicinity, searching for a parent. This child was too young to be out so far alone. She knew many children took swimming lessons, but no matter how well he swam, he shouldn't be unsupervised.

The child tried to stand on the float toy, lost his balance, and fell off. As the float toy bounced away atop the surface of the water, the little boy screamed and flailed his arms and legs. He started to go under.

Roberta hurried to him and grabbed onto his little arm, pulling him out of the water. The child still kicked wildly and waved his arms.

"It's okay! I've got you!" she tried to call over his yelling. "Calm down! You're fine now!" Frantically, Roberta tried to get a grip on his thrashing body with her other hand.

The child continued to thrash and scream. If he would settle down, she could still hold him up and reach for his float toy to try to calm him. She carried him into more shallow water and left the stupid toy to float away.

She dearly hoped someone on the beach would come to help her, but there was no one on the shore. Out of the corner of her eye, she finally saw a man approaching. He grabbed the child roughly from her arms, ignored her, and swore at the little boy as he gave the little fellow a resounding smack, making the child scream even louder.

She was about to rebuke the man for allowing the child to go into the deep water unsupervised when he turned, belched in her face, and made a crude comment. The stench of liquor almost made her gag as he stepped closer. One hand reached forward, and she noticed the tattoo on his wrist. Roberta stepped back as quickly as she could in the water.

The crude man stepped forward again, closer this time, as he repositioned the crying little boy in one arm, continuing to leer at her. She didn't know what to do and was ready to start screaming when Garrett, fully dressed, appeared in the water beside the man.

His lips drawn into a tight line, cheeks rigid, he stood within a foot of the disgusting man. The child screamed louder. For a second, Roberta worried Garrett was going to hit the man. Instead, Garrett crossed his arms, squared his shoulders, and clenched his fists tight. "Apologize to the lady. And you had better thank her for saving the child."

Instead of apologizing, the man yelled a string of obscenities in Garrett's face.

"That does it. Out of the water and get off the beach." Garrett straightened to his full height, towering over the rude man by at least three or four inches. The wet shirt clung to his muscular body, emphasizing his height and the width of his powerful shoulders. Roberta sure wouldn't have dared cross him.

The man continued to swear and stomped out of the water, carrying the still-screaming child. Garrett followed him to the water's edge and stood defiantly on the shoreline, watching the man pick up his belongings and pull the child roughly by the hand down the path to the campsites.

Garrett walked to an untidy pile at the water's edge containing his boots and socks and his walkie-talkie. He spoke into it briefly, touched his soaking wet shorts and the clip on his belt where the unit usually rested, then held it in his hand instead.

Garrett handed her a towel. "Let's go sit down at the picnic table and we'll put our shoes and socks back on."

By the time they reached the table, her feet were dry. They sat side by side as Roberta pulled on her socks and sneakers, then waited for Garrett to lace his hiking boots. He neatly folded the tops of his wool socks over the rims of the boots, picked up his walkie-talkie, and they walked to the path leading back to the campsites in silence.

His shorts had stopped dripping, but were still soaking wet. They hung on him like wet rags, and his scuffed boots were dark from the water. Compared to the pristine ranger of this morning, his bedraggled appearance almost sent her into a burst of giggles.

"I've got to get some dry clothes, then get back on duty. If it's any consolation to you, I logged this, and I'll be filing an official report. Any minor infraction, and his group will be asked to leave."

"Thank you, Garrett." She didn't know what else to say.

He raised his hand, resting his fingers on her cheek. His head lowered, and she thought he was going to kiss her, but instead, his eyebrows knotted above the sunglasses and he studied her face, as best she could tell through the dark lenses. "Are you sure you're all right?"

Roberta leaned into his hand, finding strange comfort in the roughness of his fingers against her soft cheek. She shuffled her feet to bring herself slightly closer to him, until she could sense the cool dampness radiating from him. Part of her wanted him to kiss her. Oddly shaken by the thought, she quickly rationalized it away. This latest incident must have upset her more than she realized. "You've asked me that more times in the last twenty-four hours than I can count."

He let out a sad little laugh. "Do these kind of disasters happen often to you?"

"Never."

He shook his head as he gently ran his thumb along her temple. "I feel like this was my fault. If I had been there, watching, it wouldn't have happened."

It probably wouldn't have, but it didn't make any difference.

It wasn't his fault, and she couldn't let him accept responsibility. She was about to reassure him when his walkie-talkie beeped. His hand dropped, and she immediately missed it.

"Excuse me." He flipped the switch and turned his head to speak into it. "Lamont."

Garrett held the unit to his ear, but she could still hear the caller's voice. "We followed him like you said, and we've got him. Site 45. Left the fire at a full burn while he was gone, and there's open liquor everywhere. Soon as you get here, we can evict him. Come on down."

"I'm on my way," Garrett replied. His hand reached to the clip on his belt, but instead of clipping his walkie-talkie to it, he pulled his hand away when his fingers brushed the dampness. He held the unit at his side. "Gotta go. I'll be back when I can."

With that, he turned and left.

six

Roberta was alone for the rest of the afternoon.

She had no idea if it was unusual for someone to be kicked out of a campground, but she didn't think so. She couldn't tell if the victory made her proud or angry with Garrett. On the other hand, having such a pig get kicked out and his weekend ruined gave her a tremendous amount of satisfaction. A stab of guilt then got the better of her, because as a Christian, she was supposed to forgive the man. She'd have to work on that.

As she awaited Molly and her friend's arrival, she planned to ask Molly about Garrett and try to find out what Molly could have said to cause him to stick to her like glue.

Settling slowly and gently into the hammock with her book under her chin, Roberta prepared to enjoy the rest of the afternoon. At first she smiled, knowing Garrett wouldn't come near her as long as she had the book in her hand, but then she kicked herself for thinking such a thing. Over the breakfast table, before he put his sunglasses on, she saw the slight discoloration of the bruise on his cheek, and she hoped no one, especially the other rangers, had seen it. She would have to make it up to him somehow, and maybe Molly could give her a suggestion, if she could admit to Molly how it happened. She picked up her book.

The sound of a car stopping in front of the campsite woke Roberta up. She opened her eyes and focused as Molly walked into the campsite. Slipping more gently out of the hammock this time, she ran to greet Molly.

"Molly! I'm so glad to see you! How's your mom?"

Molly sighed, then shrugged her shoulders. "She's fine, but it really scared me that time. I thought I should stay at home last night, you know. How was your night in the wilderness? I asked Garrett to keep an eye on you. Has he been around a few times?"

A *few* times? She should be so lucky.

"Come on, we're going to unload the boat first."

"Boat?" She followed Molly back up to the entranceway to see a large canoe strapped to the top of Molly's friend's car, and a small utility trailer behind it, filled with boxes, oars, and camping paraphernalia.

"Robbie, have you ever met Gwen before?"

Gwen waved from behind the wheel. Considering they were twins, she didn't look that much like Garrett. While they shared the family resemblance, Gwen's features were much finer. While not delicate, Gwen was beautiful, if not drop-dead gorgeous. And thin. And probably tall, too. And her smile could have lit a banquet hall. Robbie smiled politely as Molly introduced them.

They followed a path that said restricted use only, but Gwen assured her they had Garrett's permission to be there. The smooth pristine lake stretched out before them, and a small dock jutted into the water. Roberta stood back as Molly and Gwen heaved the canoe off the top of the car. Roberta stood back to watch, because they looked like they knew what they were doing, and she didn't want to get in the way. Gwen was as tall as Roberta thought she'd be.

Gwen tied the canoe securely to the dock, and they returned to their campsite. Unpacking the trailer quickly, they agreed to make coffee before starting supper. As they sat down, Molly grinned at Roberta. "So, what do you think of Garrett? He kind of keeps to himself, so this job in the middle of nowhere is perfect for him."

Keeps to himself? Were they thinking of the same man? Roberta opened her mouth to ask, but Molly didn't give her a chance to get a word out.

"Look, there's a big rock on the table, with a piece of paper under it." Molly threw the rock into the bush and picked up the note. "It's from Garrett. Look at his handwriting, I swear it gets worse every time I see it. No wonder he likes this job—no paperwork." She briefly held the paper in front of Roberta's face, as if that would give her time to analyze it, then snatched it back when Roberta held out her hand. "It says, 'I WANTED TO CHECK UP ON YOU, BUT YOU WERE ARMED SO I DIDN'T WAKE YOU.'" Molly shook the paper, then looked at Roberta. "Hey, what's this all about?"

Roberta blushed. She grabbed the paper out of Molly's hand, crumpled it up, and threw it into the fire pit. "Nothing," she mumbled. "Absolutely nothing."

Gwen thunked her coffee cup on the wooden picnic table. "I don't know about you guys, but I'm starved. This fresh air always makes me hungry. I'm going to start supper." Gwen fetched some newspaper out of the trunk of her car, crumpled it up, and piled some kindling and larger logs on top of it in the fire pit. "I see you have a good pile of wood and kindling here. Did you manage okay by yourself, Robbie?"

"Oh, yes, Garrett helped me carry the firewood, then chopped up all this kindling for me."

Molly and Gwen looked at each other.

"I'm glad Garrett helped you," Gwen cleared her throat, then spoke in a more normal tone. "You did a good job setting up the tent trailer, too. Did it take you long?"

"Probably. I'm not sure how long it usually takes, but Garrett helped with the hard parts."

Gwen hesitated for an almost indiscernible moment. "Oh. I see you got Garrett's hammock up. Comfortable, isn't it? You were sleeping when we got here, weren't you?"

"Yes, I was out like a light. Although I am embarrassed to admit that the first time I tried it I fell out. Garrett showed me the right way to get in and out without hurting myself."

Gwen stopped playing with the wood and turned her head. It almost looked like she was going to say something, but instead she turned back to the task at hand and struck a match, holding it to the paper.

The three of them busied themselves and barbecued a

good supper over the fire. The dishes were nearly done when Roberta heard familiar heavy footsteps approaching in the gravel.

"Good evening, ladies."

Gwen and Molly gaily chorused together, "Hi, Garrett!"

Roberta grunted.

"Enjoy your supper?"

"Naturally. I cooked it," Gwen replied. "Have you eaten?"

"Yup."

"Good," she continued. "Because we didn't save you any."

Everyone laughed except Roberta.

"The place is full, as I expected. The naturalist phoned in sick, so I'm going to have to do the programs this weekend. I won't have much, if any, free time. In fact, I have to get moving right now to go set up."

Knowing he started at dawn, Roberta wondered if he was normally expected to work these kind of hours. She remembered reading some literature posted in various locations about information programs and slide shows to be presented throughout the weekend at varying times every day. Some of them had sounded very interesting, and judging from her one-sided conversation with Garrett on the path to and from the beach, he possessed a good knowledge about the flora and fauna of the area.

Gwen laughed out loud. "Maybe we'll go sit in the back and heckle you."

Garrett frowned. "Better not."

"Okay, we'll sit in the front."

Garrett said nothing, but his frown deepened. Gwen smiled widely and pushed him on the arm. He stood solid as a rock. "Try and stop us."

Molly joined her teasing. "I'm starting to think of a million questions already."

Garrett remained silent.

Gwen continued. "Lighten up. Don't you want a cheering section?"

"No."

"How about a fan club? Doesn't that sound like fun?"

All he did was give his sister a dirty look.

Finally, Roberta couldn't stand it. In a way she felt sorry for him. It sounded like his sister was planning on embarrassing him in front of the campers. How would anyone respect his authority as a park ranger if he was being harassed during a presentation? "I think we can find something else to do, don't you?"

Gwen sighed loudly. "Oh, all right. I'll behave, but under protest."

"Thank you," Garrett grumbled, and he turned around and left.

Gwen grumbled the entire time while the three of them washed the dishes, but her smile gave her away. "I'd been looking forward to pestering him, but I'm not going to do it alone. Maybe as Robbie gets to know him better, she'll see Garrett needs a little convincing to come out of his shell."

Molly giggled. "Forget it; he's a lost cause. Besides, I think Robbie needs some time to herself for a while."

Roberta had been listening as she stacked the dishes in their respective plastic boxes. Shell? Garrett needed to come out of his shell? Lost in thought, she missed part of the conversation.

"Are you coming?"

Roberta looked at them. "What? Where?"

"To Garrett's presentation. We only promised to behave. We didn't promise not to go. Come on."

She really had wanted to learn a little about the animals and natural phenomena of the area, but not at Garrett's expense. "I don't think so."

"Come on," Molly said, waving her hand to try to convince her. "It's going to start soon. The flyer said tonight it was a slide show all about the local parks. It's going to be interesting. We were planning on going even if Garrett wasn't going to be the one doing it."

"Oh, all right. Why do I let you do this to me?"

Molly laughed. "Because I know what's best."

"Not likely."

Upon their arrival at the small amphitheater, Gwen sat center front, Molly sat beside Gwen, and Roberta sat beside Molly. Garrett kept glancing at them nervously but said nothing, which Roberta thought was unusual, but a welcome change. Since it was already dusk, he wasn't wearing the sunglasses. With only the hat on, she was caught off guard by how handsome he was in his uniform, his good looks slightly marred by the slight discoloration on his cheek. She suspected that Gwen wouldn't lose a chance to tease him about it, and since she hadn't yet, she must not have noticed.

For a while she watched as he smiled and chatted with the campers surrounding him, answering their questions. She also noticed most of them were female.

More and more people arrived, until the small amphitheater was almost full. Garrett started his presentation with a little speech, showing a map of the local provincial parks, and then moved on to a slide show, where he gave a short explanation about each picture shown.

After the slide show, he elaborated on the presentation and asked if there were any questions. When all the questions were answered, he thanked everyone for coming and encouraged everyone to take advantage of all the features and activities provided by the Parks and Recreation Department. As he sent everyone on his way, Roberta thought he'd have made a good teacher.

She was anxious to leave him alone, but Gwen and Molly wanted to stay. Having seen enough of him in the last day and a half to last a lifetime, Roberta returned to the campsite alone, grateful she had brought her flashlight. She remembered the hard way how very, very dark it got at night with no streetlights or glow from the city. After piling everything up to start another fire, she fetched the lantern. She was in the midst of searching the camper for the matches, when she heard the footsteps of someone entering the campsite, crunching in the gravel.

Her hand froze on the drawer. Molly and Gwen's chattering and laughter would be heard long before she heard their footsteps, and Garrett would either be with them or well behind them, needing to wait until his audience left and the projector and other paraphernalia were packed away and returned to ranger headquarters.

She doubted it would be another park ranger.

Already on her hands and knees from picking through the cupboard, she flicked off her flashlight and stayed low, slowly lifting her head to peek through the corner of the window.

It was a man. It wasn't Garrett. And it wasn't a ranger. All the valuables were locked in the cars, so if it was a would-be thief, he would get nothing. Hopefully he wouldn't check the camper.

The man didn't go near the cars. He walked into the center of the site and looked around. "Hey, little darling," he called out, "where are you?"

That voice! She dropped to her hands and knees as her stomach churned. It was the same man who approached her last night at the outhouse. But he hadn't called her "darling" then, the only one who had called her that was Garrett, in his dreams.

Her mind raced. It wasn't a raccoon last night, it was him! He had come in to the campsite in the middle of the night, expecting her to be alone.

Roberta covered her mouth with her hand to prevent herself from screaming. She prayed he wouldn't look in the dark camper and find her cowering on the floor. The flashlight in her hand could be used as a weapon as a last resort, but she doubted she'd be very effective against a man that size, or any man, for that matter. At only five-foot-four, she wasn't much threat to anything or anybody. Even the four-year-old child had gotten the better of her. Why hadn't she taken those self-defense courses advertised in the newspaper last fall?

After what seemed an eternity, his steps retreated and disappeared.

She knelt to peek out the window to be sure he was gone. Her heart pounded and her hands shook as she slowly opened the door and poked her head out, an inch at a time. Searching the area slowly, she exited the camper when she was sure he was truly gone.

Panic started to overtake her. She couldn't stay here! She wanted to bolt and go home, but Molly had her keys in her pocket, so that wasn't an option. Flashlight in hand, she fled the campsite and ran to where she hoped everyone else would still be.

ﾐ&

After all the campers left the amphitheater, Garrett packed everything up. He closed the lid on the last box as Gwen and Molly chatted with another ranger.

Out of the corner of his eye, Garrett saw Robbie running toward him at a breakneck pace. Her wide eyes showed fear, and her abrupt halt as she skidded on the cement beside him spoke frenzy. His breath caught as she grabbed his arm and started shaking it.

She gulped for breath so badly he barely made her words out. "A man. . .outhouse. . .raccoon. . .looking for. . .hid in. . . went away. . ."

"Calm down, Robbie," he tried to speak slowly and softly, but his heart hammered in his chest. "Take a deep breath and tell me, slowly, what's wrong."

She squeezed her eyes shut, then opened them wide. Garrett rested his hands on her shoulders and waited. From the way she couldn't catch her breath, it looked like she had run the entire way from the campsite to the amphitheater.

Molly came running. "Robbie! What's wrong? Are you hurt?"

Roberta swallowed hard as her gasping subsided. Garrett could hear the tension in her voice as she spoke. "That man from last night. He came into the campsite looking for me. He called me 'darling' just like you did. It wasn't a raccoon, you idiot!" she screamed. She thumped his hands off her shoulders and settled her fists on her hips. "I was all alone hiding in the camper, terrified! I couldn't stay there so I ran here."

Garrett opened his mouth to speak, but she started up again. She grabbed one of his arms, and shook it again and continued to shout at a slightly lower volume level, but her voice was still raised and tight and rapid. "Even I could tell it wasn't a raccoon. How could you be so stupid! Can't you tell the difference? Even I could tell it was footsteps! Why did I let you convince me it was a raccoon?"

Totally ignoring their audience, Garrett trapped her hands between his forearm, which she held like a steel trap, and his hand. He lowered his voice to speak slowly and evenly. "Listen to me. I knew it wasn't a raccoon. I can certainly tell the difference between an animal and a human. I didn't want you to be frightened. I made sure to speak loudly so he would know you weren't alone and he wouldn't bother you again. Do you understand that?"

He paused long enough for his words to sink in. Robbie nodded.

"When we went to the outhouse I radioed the rangers and told them to be on the lookout for a prowler, but they couldn't find him. You have to trust me, Robbie. I did what I thought was best so he wouldn't think you were all by yourself. Just don't go off by yourself again until we find out who he is."

"Okay." She nodded again, and he allowed her to pull her hands away. "I won't go anywhere by myself."

Molly stood to the side, gawking. "Come on," she said, "let's all go back. No one will bother us if the three of us stick together."

Garrett didn't like the three of them camping alone, but there was nothing he could do about it. "With one man short, I'm going to have to stay at the ranger camp for the weekend."

Gwen stepped in. "Don't worry about us, Bro, we'll be fine. Safety in numbers."

Roberta stared at the ground.

Molly touched her shoulder. "Let's go back now. I've got some popcorn that I can hear calling me. Come on, Gwen."

Gwen nodded and said a quick good-bye to the ranger she was talking with.

Garrett had turned his back to lift the boxes when he heard Gwen's voice behind him.

"Darling? Last night? What exactly was going on last night?"

"None of your business," he grumbled, balancing the boxes so he could carry them all in one trip. He steadied the pile and walked to the truck, ignoring his sister.

He shuffled the boxes in the truck bed, watching the three of them walk down the dark road, three flashlight beams zigzagging across the road as they made their way. What was he going to do? As much as Robbie felt singled out by the prowler, in all likelihood, the prowler would act the same with any lone woman. The thought didn't ease his mind.

He knew he should be out walking around the campsite, keeping an eye out for trouble, but his heart told him to stay in site 27 with his sister, Molly, and Robbie, to keep an eye out for them, even though it wasn't likely they'd be bothered.

Being Friday night, if anyone was going to get drunk and disorderly, tonight would be the night. Already the rangers had kicked out one undesirable group. Well on their way to drunken oblivion, they had a car full of beer and half-empty liquor bottles littered all over the site, when the other rangers approached them about leaving a roaring campfire unattended. And, if he was not mistaken, he had detected the smoke from a hastily butted joint. That group was trouble looking for a place to happen, and it wasn't going to happen at his campground. As good as it felt to tell them to leave, he would have derived more satisfaction punching the guy's lights out for harassing Robbie, but as a peace officer and park representative, he couldn't. He needed to work this out with God, but for now, the picture in his mind of the man reaching out to grab Robbie made him see red.

Garrett shoved the last box roughly to the front of the truck bed. He had to get started making the rounds, checking up on the campsites, although he'd never felt less like it. If he was being honest with himself, he would admit that the real reason he wanted to join the three of them was to talk to Robbie, even though she'd made it quite plain that she didn't want to talk to him.

He was a glutton for punishment. As soon as most of the campers turned in for the night and he could make arrangements, he knew where he was going.

seven

Gwen and Molly burst into peals of laughter at another of their jokes. Roberta just smiled. With fresh, though slightly burnt popcorn and a large pitcher of icy Kool-Aid, they sat around the campfire, huddled in their jackets, telling jokes and behaving as she thought typical campers would behave. She only half listened as Gwen started in on another joke, with Molly butting in and trying to guess the punch line.

She'd called him stupid. She'd taken all her frustrations out on poor Garrett. He hadn't deserved that. And he never said a thing, he'd taken it all in stride. Neither had he brought up about her hitting him in the face with her book. Even if no one else noticed the bruise, she knew it was there. Fortunately neither Molly nor Gwen had said anything yet, at least not that she knew of.

Gwen and Molly roared with laughter again, so much that neither of them heard the sound of the Parks Department truck or the crunching of footsteps in the gravel. Roberta did.

"Hi! Did anyone save me some?"

Gwen and Molly jumped, spilling their popcorn, then laughed even louder. Roberta stared at the ground.

Molly stuck her tongue out. "Make your own. You and your ranger buddies spend more time sitting around goofing off than doing any real work anyhow. I know what you really do all day. Nothing."

Garrett grinned. "Think what you want. It's hard work handing out maps and pointing out the signs that lead to the nature trails all day." He smiled so wide that his dimples appeared and his teeth shone in the flickering glow of the campfire.

Gwen threw a handful of popcorn at him. He never lost his grin.

"Gotta go. Catch you next round." Garrett started to walk to the truck, but Roberta didn't want the earlier incident hanging over her head. She ran after him.

"Garrett! Wait!"

He stopped with one hand resting on the truck's door handle. "Yes, Robbie?"

She stood beside him, but she couldn't face him. She stared at the ground, knowing by now he'd seen a lot of the top of her head.

"I'm sorry about earlier. I know you did what you thought was best, and you were right. I apologize."

"It's okay, Robbie, I know you were upset."

She cringed. That's all he'd seen of her was upset. And she didn't like it. Normally a friendly, happy-go-lucky person, no one she knew would equate the Roberta Garland of the last couple of days with the Roberta Garland they already knew. Or would they? Nothing had ever gone wrong in her life before; in fact, she'd coasted happily along from day to day without any hindrances or stumbling blocks in her path. If this was the way she behaved when troubles happened, then maybe she didn't know herself, either.

"Is that it? I've got to get back to work, Robbie."

She raised her head and blinked dumbly up at him. "Uh, yes," she mumbled, nodding as she spoke. She almost turned around, but his smile stopped her. One day, the woman he called "darling" for real would be a very lucky woman. But instead of daydreaming about Garrett's future, she had some serious thinking to do about her own.

"See you next round, then." He gripped the brim of his hat, tipped his head slightly forward, and drove away slowly, looking for whatever it was that rangers looked for.

With that burden lifted, she returned to the campfire, but she continued to think about Garrett, much to her dismay. Not only had she questioned his intelligence and his judgment, she'd done it in front of his sister and Molly, and also within earshot of several other campers. Garrett was the local authority, the camp police, so to speak, and from the way he talked about the other rangers, he seemed to rank above them. Yet, he'd forgiven her in a flash. If the situation had been reversed, would she have done the same? She doubted it.

Molly and Gwen bantered jokes back and forth, and Roberta only listened with one ear while she thought about Garrett. After one particular loud burst of laughter, Gwen suggested they pack things up for the night. Roberta readily agreed. She knew the hard way that morning came early in the middle of nowhere.

She poured water on the fire while Molly and Gwen poked around in the embers. The wood hissed as the water touched it, and all three of them stood clear of the steam.

Obviously not wanting to go to bed, Molly grumbled. "When I'm camping, why do I wake up earlier than my alarm clock?"

Gwen nodded. "I know. Happens to me, too."

Roberta nodded as well. "Yes, we were up early this morning, too."

Molly and Gwen exchanged glances. "We?" they asked in unison.

Roberta blinked and looked at them. "Yes, Garrett and I were up at dawn. He had to go to work." She was about to complain how he left her all alone to do the dishes, but stopped. Molly's and Gwen's sticks remained planted in the ashes as they stared at her like she'd grown another head. "Why are you looking at me like that? We weren't the only ones up at that hour."

"Garrett spent the night with you? Here?" Gwen asked, lifting the stick out of the ashes.

Roberta gulped. "In his tent." She'd done nothing wrong. "Well, he said Molly asked him to keep an eye on me. When some weirdo scared me, I guess he took it upon himself to be my guardian angel or something. To tell the truth, I was glad he did, because someone came into the campsite in the middle of the night, but Garrett scared him off."

They said nothing, but continued to stare, eyes wide and completely motionless. Roberta glanced back and forth between the two of them, then averted her gaze to study what was left of the fire. "He seems to have attached himself to me. Every time I turn around, he seems to show up again."

Gwen's and Molly's eyes opened wider.

Roberta held the bucket tighter. "What? Why are you two staring at me like that?"

"You're talking about Garrett, right? My brother, the ranger guy who was just here?"

"Of course I know who Garrett is, Gwen! I've certainly seen enough of him over the last couple of days."

"Wow." Gwen turned her head toward the entrance to the campsite, the last place they had seen Garrett, then back to Roberta. "He's usually pretty shy and tends to keep to himself."

"Could have fooled me," Roberta mumbled. "I wish he would leave me alone." She hadn't asked for him to check up on her constantly. But in the end, she was glad he did.

Molly yawned. "Forget it; let's get ready for bed. One last trip to the outhouse, and we can change."

After their trip, they locked themselves in the camper. Molly started to giggle. "I feel like a teenager having a slumber party. What we need now is a big pizza, loaded with everything so we can get indigestion and then sit and talk all night."

"No thanks," Roberta moaned.

"Oh, Robbie, you're such a party pooper!"

"Molly, we're going to be sleeping together in this little thing for a week and a half! If we're going to be doing whatever it is that campers do, why in the world would we stay up all night and talk if we're going to be together night and day? Don't you think we'll get a little sick of each other?"

"No way! We're party animals!"

Roberta snorted. "Good night." She pulled the top of the

sleeping bag up to her chin. "Party without me."

Before Roberta fell asleep, she heard either Molly or Gwen snoring. So much for their party.

They all managed to sleep well past sunrise. They enjoyed Roberta's cereal for breakfast, and after taking a remarkably long time to wash three bowls and three spoons, they were ready for some action.

Following much discussion, they decided to observe Garrett at the amphitheater. The morning's schedule promised a nature talk about the animals native to the area. Much of his speech Roberta had already heard on the path to the beach, but she sat and listened politely.

Even still, he managed to pique her interest. In addition to an entertaining and informative presentation, Garrett displayed pictures of the animals, described and drew their footprints, and then encouraged all the campers to try to find some animal tracks and figure out what kind of animal made them. He named a few good places to check out, and opened the floor for questions. Caught up in the excitement of the crowd, when the presentation was over, she felt confident enough to enter the trails and go hunting for tracks.

Gwen wanted to stay and talk to Garrett when everything was done, because although they lived in the same house when he wasn't staying at the ranger camp, she hadn't seen much of him lately. Molly didn't want to listen to Garrett and Gwen's private conversation, so Roberta took the opportunity to drag Molly onto the nearest nature trail to begin their adventure of discovery.

They were considerably farther down the path before Molly finally developed a little enthusiasm. Bending over and scanning the ground, both of them searched for evidence of animal habitation.

Try as they might, Roberta and Molly couldn't find anything. Molly gave up first, and picked a fallen tree to sit on. "Haven't you given up yet?" she called, not trying at all to keep the boredom out of her voice.

"No. I was feeding the squirrels around here yesterday. They had to leave some footprints, don't you think?"

"You mean I've been hanging around here when all you've been doing is searching for lousy squirrel footprints? You've got to be kidding!" Molly stood, ready to return to the campsite.

"Molly!" Roberta scolded good-naturedly. "Sit down. I know they were here, so there have to be some footprints. I'm going to turn into a nature lover, you wait and see."

"Hmph. I won't hold my breath."

"Quit being so. . .Molly!" she exclaimed. "Look! I found something! Right here! Footprints!" Roberta tried her hardest not to jump up and down. Success!

Molly wasn't as enthusiastic. Slowly, she shuffled her way to the tracks that held Roberta's rapt attention. She rubbed her chin as she examined the neat set of tracks. "Those are too big for a squirrel."

"Well, Garrett said there are lots of rodents and the like out here. But this is one of the tracks he drew. Think. What kind of animals did he mention?"

Molly tilted her head as she thought. "Chipmunk? No, that would be the same size as the squirrel. Coyote? No, this is a rodent, too small for a coyote."

Roberta tapped her foot and put a finger up to her chin as well, to help her think. "What else did he draw? Raccoon? No, that was narrow. Hold on, I think I remember, it's a. . ."

They looked at each in horror.

"Skunk!" they hollered in unison. They screeched and ran down the trail back to the campsite as fast as their legs would carry them.

≥∙

Garrett leaned his head back and laughed. He could picture the scene Gwen had just described, imagining their mother struggling to handle the situation. Just when his laughter subsided enough to speak, Molly broke into the clearing in a breakneck run, full speed, arms waving, screaming his name, with Robbie close behind.

His stomach clenched. Both of them looked like they had seen a dead body. Ignoring Gwen in midsentence, he jumped to his feet and bolted off to meet them. "What's wrong? What happened?"

Molly's chest heaved as she gasped for air, holding one hand up to her throat. "Garrett! In the bush! On the trail! It's. . .it's. . ."

Garrett hoped she wasn't going to be sick. After all the things that happened around Robbie, it could be anything."

Robbie managed to blurt it out first. "Skunk!" she wheezed. With her arm outstretched, she pointed to the entrance of the trail as she puffed. "Over there. . .by the tree. . ."

Garrett's breath came out in a rush. He hadn't even realized he'd been holding it in. "That's it? You saw a skunk?" He bent his head and pinched the bridge of his nose with his thumb and forefinger. "A skunk?" he asked again, in complete disbelief. "You almost gave me heart failure over a little skunk?" He shook his head, still holding the bridge of his nose. One of these days. . .

Robbie regained enough breath to stop gasping for air as she spoke. "We didn't actually see it, but we found its footprints, just like you drew." She continued to point to the path, staring with her eyes wide, as if she expected the wild killer creature to appear and maim and destroy them all.

Garrett covered his face with his hands and groaned, trying to contain himself. "You mean you didn't even see it?" He hated campers like this. It could have been days ago the skunk was there if all they saw was tracks.

Robbie's arm dropped to her side. "It was there! I know it! A skunk! It could have attacked us!"

Garrett lifted his face out of his hands. Robbie's eyes still held the wild fear of a frightened doe. He tried to speak slowly, evenly, and calmly. "Skunks do not attack people. Skunks are timid animals. If a skunk sees a human, it runs one way and the person runs the other way. They're more afraid of you than you are of them. The only thing they do is spray, and they only spray when threatened. Did you threaten the poor little animal that wasn't even there?"

Robbie and Molly's faces reddened. "Oh," Robbie mouthed. She and Molly turned and looked at each other like bad children who got caught with their fingers in the cookie jar. "Then maybe your next nature talk should include what to do if you see a skunk." She made a sad pathetic little laugh, then backed up.

Garrett didn't laugh. He didn't say anything. He pressed his lips together tightly to avoid saying something he would regret. At least Molly should have known better. Molly had been camping before.

The corners of Robbie's lips curved up for a split second in a quick grin, probably meant to disarm him, then dropped. "Maybe I'd better go back to the campsite now. Anyone coming with me? Molly?"

Molly took one look at him, glanced back at Robbie, then nodded. "Yes, I think I forgot to turn off the television," she said in a timid little voice, not like Molly at all. "We had better go right now."

Garrett glared at them, standing frozen to the spot, his hands planted firmly on his hips as they hustled down the path leading to the campsites.

"What was that all about?"

He turned to see Gwen scowling back at him in a pose identical to his own.

"What do you want?" he barked.

"Who bit you?" she snapped back. "Why in the world did you get so mad at them? They're inexperienced!" She waved one hand in the air, then planted it back on her hip. "They were genuinely afraid of getting attacked by a wild animal!"

They stared at each other in silence as her words sunk in. Why did he get so angry? An agitated sigh escaped. He knew Robbie didn't know the least little bit about wild animals, and Molly wasn't much better. No doubt about it, they had totally overreacted, but then, so had he. Never again did he want to experience the soul-wrenching terror that something wrong had really happened to her this time.

Getting blasted by his sister did a good job of defusing his anger. He shrugged his shoulders. "To tell the truth, I don't know," he said lamely.

"What do you mean, you don't know?" Gwen tapped her foot.

Garrett threw his hands up in the air, then dropped them to his sides. "Give me a break. You're acting like Mom when we were little kids. I don't owe you an explanation!"

"Yes you do! Molly is my friend, and Roberta is our guest."

"And she's been nothing but a pain since she got here." He tried not to shout but failed. He waved one arm in the air in the direction they'd last walked. "Every time I turn around, she's either doing something wrong, hurting herself, or she's got some creep or weirdo after her. Now she thinks she's about to be attacked by some poor defenseless animal that wasn't even in the vicinity! Women!"

Without waiting for a response, Garrett turned and stomped off, leaving Gwen standing alone in the middle of the empty amphitheater with her mouth hanging open.

❧

Roberta stuck the knife deep into the peanut butter jar, diligently helping Molly prepare lunch as they both worked in complete silence. She'd made a fool of herself in front of him. Again.

They'd made a big deal out of nothing, but really, they hadn't known any better. What if a wild skunk had appeared out of the bush? What if they had frightened it, and it had attacked them? What if. . .

"Peanut butter sandwiches, my favorite." Gwen's voice broke her train of thought. It was just as well.

Conversation was slow to get started, and they all carefully avoided any subject matter relating to wild animals or Garrett, but soon Molly and Gwen were laughing and joking once more, while Roberta listened and smiled politely.

"So," Gwen mumbled around a mouthful of sticky peanut butter, then noisily gulped her drink to wash it down, "what are we going to do on this lovely sunny afternoon?"

Molly looked up at the sky, then glanced between Roberta and Gwen. "I know; let's go for a swim. The beach here is really nice, Robbie. Lots of nice soft sand."

"Hmph," Roberta grumbled. "I'm not interested. I've already seen the beach."

"You have? You told me you'd never been here before."

"Yesterday. Garrett took me to the beach."

Gwen's head shot up. "Garrett? He was working yesterday."

"I know. He said he had beach duty, so he took me to the beach. It's very nice. Clean and well cared for." She smiled as Gwen and Molly stared blankly at her. "And they're really strict about no dogs allowed. When I was swimming, he kicked someone with a dog off the beach." She neglected to tell them the rest, especially how he ran into the water fully dressed to save her virtue.

Molly shrugged her shoulders.

Roberta felt the heat rising into her cheeks. "A little boy fell off his float toy yesterday. I pulled him up out of the water, but his father was, well, he wasn't very nice to me. Garrett, well, he helped me again."

"What did Garrett do?"

Roberta's finger drew little circles in the layer of ash that had blown onto the picnic table. She'd never forget her shock at seeing Garrett appear in the water fully dressed, the expression on his face when he ordered the boy's father to apologize, or her impression that he was going to deck the guy.

"Oh, he got them kicked out."

"Kicked out?" Gwen asked, her eyes almost bugging out of her head.

"Wow. . ." Molly's voice trailed off.

"Well," Gwen said, "if Garrett kicked the guy out yesterday, he won't be there to bother you again."

"I guess."

"Well, want to go again, then? It's a nice hot sunny day," Molly said.

Molly and Gwen cleaned up and then they scurried into the camper to change.

The beach was crowded.

"It wasn't like this yesterday." Roberta turned her head to scan the entire beach, milling about with people. They'd be hard-pressed to find a spot to lay all three towels side by side and still have a little privacy. "Yesterday there couldn't have been more than a dozen people here. And one dog. And he wasn't here long."

After finding a spot to lay out their towels, they raced to the shoreline to wet their toes. Gwen and Molly shivered and backed up. "Oooh! It's so cold!" they complained.

"Last one in's a rotten egg!" shouted Roberta as she sprinted in until she could no longer run, and then she dove. Rising out of the waist-deep water, she swooshed her wet hair off her face as she stood and turned to the shore. "Cowards!" she yelled.

Her mouth stayed open long after no sound came out. Standing alongside Molly and Gwen was Garrett. She wondered what he was doing there, and if he had been watching her. When he saw he had her attention, he waved.

"Hi! I'm on beach duty again," he called out, as if he heard her thoughts.

Roberta frowned, not moving from her safe position waist-deep in the water. "Just run in; you're only torturing yourselves by inching in."

Garrett smiled and waved, leaving Gwen and Molly alone on the shore as he sauntered slowly down the beach and into the picnic area.

Despite her instructions, Molly and Gwen continued to inch their way in, cringing every time they got a little deeper. Finally Roberta couldn't stand it. She ran and flopped down on her stomach in front of them, spraying them with a cascade of water, causing them to throw up their hands and screech.

"No fair!" shouted Gwen. "You're already wet!"

Gwen splashed her in the face, then Roberta splashed back, getting Molly in the face. The three of them laughed and splashed each other like little kids, squealing and splashing, until they heard a voice.

"Excuse me, ladies."

They all froze. Garrett stood on the shore, his arms folded across his chest, looking every inch the authoritative Mr. Ranger. "I have to ask you ladies to stop splashing. You're disturbing others in the water."

Red-faced, they slunk down and pushed off quietly without splashing a drop. Meeting at the rope that signaled the end of the designated swimming area, they continued their playful cavorting where no one else was near. Treading water, they splashed and laughed in private, swimming underwater and playing on the rope and buoys until they'd had enough.

Upon reaching the shore, they coated each other liberally with sunscreen, stretched out on their towels until they were warmed up, then headed back to the campsite.

Even though he was gone, all the way down the path, Roberta kept picturing Garrett as he stood on the shore in his uniform. Tall and powerful and handsome, in a rugged sort of way, even though he wore shorts, which should have looked silly on a man. He instantly had the respect of everyone on the beach, herself included.

And she couldn't get his image out of her mind.

eight

Following a delicious supper of barbecued chicken and slightly burnt potatoes, Roberta, Molly, and Gwen tried to decide what to do until nightfall. Taking a vote with two for and one against, they decided to attend Garrett's evening presentation at the amphitheater.

Grumbling all the way, Roberta tagged along, deliberately trying to slow them down, hoping if they arrived late, there wouldn't be any empty seats, and they would be forced to turn back. Or, if they were late enough, it would be too awkward to enter once Garrett started, and they would leave.

They arrived with plenty of time. Gwen and Molly headed center front, again.

Roberta watched from her seat as Molly and Gwen chatted with Garrett while he prepared his materials and the slide projector. As darkness fell, he pointed to the empty seats beside Roberta, ordering Gwen and Molly to sit down, and he called the audience's attention to begin his topic of the night, which was hiking.

Despite her bad intentions, Roberta found him fascinating, and she immensely enjoyed his presentation. Sparked with a touch of humor, he illustrated good and bad examples of a typical hiker, complete with volunteers from the audience, followed by an in-depth description of the local trails and suggested difficulty levels.

Every once in a while their eyes met, and every time it happened, Roberta's heartbeat quickened. At the conclusion of his presentation, a group of young women surrounded Garrett, vying for his attention. Rather than compete, the three of them returned to their campsite. Molly and Gwen complained about the women, but Roberta didn't care.

Gwen used the last of the kindling to build the campfire for the night. Not long after that, she threw in the last log, as well. This time, Molly and Roberta used Gwen's car, which still had the little utility trailer hooked on the back, to carry a huge pile of wood back from the stockpile.

Molly wiped her hands on the back of her jeans. "So, who gets the honors of chopping it up? Garrett cut it for you before, didn't he?"

Roberta nodded. "Yes. And he made it look so easy. I learned otherwise, the hard way."

Gwen grinned. "I know. It takes practice, and I'm probably better at it than you are, but Garrett slices through it effortlessly. Maybe next time he makes his rounds, we can sucker him into cutting us some more. I know he won't have time tomorrow, because Sunday is a busy day for him. That's when most campers leave, and all the sites have to be tidied up for the next batch. By tomorrow lunchtime, this place will be almost empty. We'll have the whole place almost to ourselves."

"Really?"

"Yes," Gwen replied, "the beach too. Usually all that's left by Sunday afternoon are a few families with little kids."

"Sounds like you know the routine. I guess you do a lot of camping."

"Yes, we do. We've camped since we were little kids, and we all loved it, but especially Garrett. It's no surprise that when he needed a job before he finishes college this is what he would choose to do."

It hadn't occurred to her that Garrett would be anything but a park ranger. "College? What's he taking?"

"Wildlife biology."

Why did she even ask?

Gwen swirled the last of her coffee in the bottom of her cup, then drank it down. "Our family used to do a lot of camping. When we got a little older, I used to especially love camping with Garrett. Because he's so big, and so, you know, staid and upright and all that, Mom and Dad trusted us off by ourselves.

I got to hang around with all his friends, and they were always extranice to me, with Garrett around."

"What's it like, having a twin brother?" Roberta didn't have any brothers or sisters, but she did have a stepsister, and while they got along fine, they were never close. She missed the camaraderie she saw between her friends and their siblings, which she had never experienced firsthand, and the easy interaction between Gwen and Garrett showed her all the more what she had missed.

Gwen poked a marshmallow onto a stick and held it over the fire. "Different than a regular brother or sister, I'm told. We used to tell each other everything. I used to think all brothers and sisters were like this, but I found out later it isn't so. We've always been really close, friends and family at the same time. If it's possible, my brother is my best friend. Sometimes I don't say a word, and he looks at me and says 'I know' and I know he knows. You know?"

Roberta smiled. "I see," she said. At least she thought she did.

The marshmallow caught fire. Molly shrieked, Gwen blew it out, blew on it some more to cool it, then popped it into her mouth.

"Yeah. And I always keep an eye out for some of the vultures that want to get their hooks on him. Sometimes it bugs him, but only a woman knows what another woman is after. He usually appreciates it a few weeks later."

Roberta wasn't sure she wanted to hear this. She tried to figure out a way to change the topic, but nothing came to her mind before Gwen started up again.

"At least out here in the middle of nowhere, he can keep to himself. He seems to like it that way."

Although Gwen had expressed that aspect of Garrett before, Roberta couldn't equate the loner Gwen described with the same Mr. Ranger who wouldn't leave her alone.

Gwen absently stabbed another marshmallow onto her stick. "Funny thing, I haven't seen him for a long time, he's been out here all summer, and I thought we'd have lots to talk about—but I think for the first time, he's holding something back."

She didn't know if she was supposed to say anything, because she really didn't know either of them, so Roberta chose to keep silent.

"We've always shared everything, but today when I started to tease him about that mark on his cheek, and I asked him who hit him, he got real silent. It was weird. I didn't know what to do."

Roberta gulped. "I did it," she mumbled, bowing her head.

"You did that? You hit my brother?"

Roberta's voice hushed to a whisper. "It was an accident. It's a long story."

"Well, now I know why he was so evasive about it."

Fortunately, the sound of approaching footsteps crunching in the gravel interrupted them.

"It's about time," Gwen called out without turning her head. "Wanna chop us some more wood? You know, help us poor defenseless campers."

"You've got to be kidding. Whatever happened to, 'Hi, good to see you'?"

"Hi. Good to see you. The ax is over there."

Garrett sat in the empty chair in front of the fire. "You'll have to feed me first."

After talking about him when he wasn't there, Roberta found it difficult to face him. Without uttering a word, she walked to Molly's car, selected something for him to eat out of the cooler in the trunk, and returned to the fireside. Very carefully, she jabbed two wieners onto a stick, and held them to the fire to cook. Studying them intently so they didn't burn, she almost didn't notice the lack of conversation around her until the silence dragged. When she turned her head, Garrett was staring at her, and Molly and Gwen were staring at Garrett.

"You're cooking them for me? You don't have to do that."

Roberta mumbled her reply, not really intending anyone to hear. She hoped no one would press her for the answer. No such luck. She raised her eyes without moving her head to see Garrett turn to glare at the other two, and when they took the hint to mind their own business, Garrett turned back to her. "I'm sorry, Robbie, I didn't hear you."

She rotated the stick to cook the other sides of the wieners. "I said, you've done so much for me, I wanted to do something for you."

It must have been a trick of the glowing firelight, but Roberta almost thought his cheeks darkened.

"I think they're done now. Here."

He accepted the hot dogs in reverent silence, not breaking eye contact. He closed his eyes for a few seconds, opened them, then still maintaining eye contact, took a big bite.

Molly's voice broke the silence. "First thing in the morning, we're going to take the canoe out. Nothing beats the early morning stillness of the lake. Then in the afternoon, we'll go swimming again."

"You ladies do know they're forecasting rain for the afternoon, don't you?"

Roberta's spirits lifted, then fell. "I guess that means swimming's off. And what in the world do you do out here in the middle of nowhere in the rain without electricity?"

Gwen merely shrugged her shoulders, undaunted. "Who cares about a little rain? We're going swimming; we're going to be wet anyway. As long as there's no lightning, it's still fun. And not only that, we'll have the entire beach to ourselves."

Roberta tried to picture it but couldn't. "I never thought of it that way."

"Gwen. I don't think—"

"Oh, Garrett. Lighten up!"

He stood. "Suit yourselves. Now I'd better chop that wood for you and get back to work."

&

Birds twittered in the treetops, muted pink and mauve clouds colored the early morning sky. Squirrels chattered in the distance, and the scent of someone's campfire brought with it the delicious smell of sizzling bacon, a vivid comparison to their own breakfast of soggy cereal in warm milk.

Roberta stood in the water up to her ankles, her pants rolled up to her knees, shivering. The lake was much warmer yesterday.

She managed to grab the second oar before it floated out of reach. It wasn't her fault they weren't fastened down properly. "Got it!" she called out, then covered her mouth with one hand. Sounds carried for miles out here in the perfect stillness. The smell of someone's breakfast meant there had to be at least a few people up at this ridiculous hour, but she doubted there were many. In fact, it was probably the rangers, not campers, who were having such an early breakfast.

Quickly, she returned to the shore and tried to pull her socks over her cold wet feet. Whose idea was this, anyway?

"Okay, Robbie, hop in, and I'll push off for you."

Roberta pulled her sweater tighter around her body. "If you don't mind, I think I'd rather watch. You two can have the first ride." After accidentally dumping the oars out so easily, she wasn't entirely sure the canoe was safe for people.

"It's not difficult."

"You two go ahead first."

"You can sit on the bottom in the middle."

She wasn't convinced the thing would safely hold three people, so Roberta shook her head.

"Suit yourself. See you in about half an hour."

"Take your time."

Roberta waved as Molly and Gwen paddled off to the center of the lake. The surface of the water shone like glass, reflecting the trees along the shore and the awakening blue of the sky above. The only disturbance to the water was the ripples caused by the oars breaking the surface, striking the water at the same time, lifting out of the water in unison. Behind them, a small wake in the shape of a narrow triangle rippled the water as the canoe sped in a silent line off into the distance.

Just before Roberta could no longer make out their individual shapes in the distance, they lifted their oars out of the water at the same time, flipped them to the other side in unison, and continued on their journey. Of course she'd seen people in canoes before, but after being involved in pushing it through the sand and into the water, she couldn't figure out how they managed to steer the thing in a straight line.

"Hi, Robbie. I expected to see you paddling off into the sunrise."

She didn't turn; she didn't have to. It was enough to feel his presence beside her as she stood surrounded by the beauty of God's creation. "Good morning, Garrett." If he'd expected her to be in the canoe with the others, she wondered why he came. She continued to take in the beauty of the scenery around her, long after the canoe disappeared around the bend. She'd never been outside to witness the latter part of a summer sunrise, or any part of the sunrise, for that matter. Maybe it was something she would have to do more often, although the big city of Vancouver never looked like this.

The quiet serenity of the moment calmed her soul like nothing else. Only a few wisps of pink clouds remained as the sky brightened. The crystal blue morning sky reflected in the perfect stillness of the lake, briefly disturbed by a duck taking off.

Out of nowhere, she heard music. For a split second she thought she'd been caught up in the Rapture, but then realized it was a guitar strumming softly behind her. When Garrett started humming quietly along with it, her breath caught at the timbre of his deep soothing voice.

"That's beautiful. Do you do this often?"

"Every Sunday. Care to join me?"

She did, without hesitation. Garrett sat on a small blanket, his legs crossed, the guitar in his lap. The brilliant early sunlight glinted off the corner of his sunglasses, but the brilliance of the glare didn't compare with his megawatt smile as she sat across the blanket from him.

Garrett sang softly, and Roberta hummed along with him, not remembering all the words. It was a song she'd sung a few times in church, but it had been a long time since she'd been, and she didn't really remember it. At that moment, she knew that had to change.

She knew the next song well, as well as the next few, so she joined him. For the last song, he picked a slow, worshipful song. Roberta closed her eyes as the words poured from her heart. She'd often heard people quote the Bible verse that where two or three were gathered together in Jesus' name, God was there in their midst. She'd agreed on the surface, but never experienced it before. This time she knew. God was there, with her and Garrett as they sat together on the blanket beside the still lake at the crack of dawn.

Garrett played the song once more, humming the melody, while mixed thoughts and words cascaded through her head. The words to the song mixed with her words of prayer as she talked to God, really talked, for the first time in a long time. It took her a while to realize that Garrett had stopped playing. For a brief minute, he held the guitar in silence, then laid it on the ground beside him. "Would you like to join me in prayer?"

"Yes," she whispered, nodding at the same time.

She could see herself in the reflection of his sunglasses. So much was she concentrating on trying to see his eyes through the dark lenses that she didn't realize he was reaching for her hands until he touched her. With both of his hands holding both of hers, he smiled gently, and they bowed their heads.

Roberta couldn't speak. But Garrett prayed enough for both of them. He praised God for the beauty around them, for each other's company, and for the salvation so freely given not only to the two of them, but to everyone who believed. Before Roberta realized that he'd changed topics, she listened to him pray for her—for the healing of her heart and soul, and for God's guidance to direct her to the perfect soul mate as her life's partner. Garrett even prayed for Mike, for forgiveness and guidance. At first she thought she'd choke, but surprised herself by realizing that she had forgiven Mike, and agreed in prayer for everything Garrett asked God on Mike's behalf. She felt cleansed and released and free.

Silent tears streamed down her cheeks as they sat without speaking, hands held, sitting cross-legged, across from each other on the blanket, heads bowed.

She didn't know how he knew the right moment, but at his mumbled, "Amen," they raised their heads and he released her hands. She scrambled to stand, but didn't back away from him. They stood toe to toe, and it was all Roberta could do to tilt her head back and gaze up to his face. Before she thought about what she was doing, she rested her hands on his waist and her forehead in the center of his chest.

"Thank you, Garrett, for including me in your private worship time today. You don't know how much I needed that." She paused to take a deep breath. "Or how good I feel about it. Thank you."

Although she certainly didn't expect a major speech from him, she didn't expect him to be totally silent. Without saying a word, he slowly and gently wrapped his arms around her and held her tight. Nestled against his huge frame, she basked in the security and protection he offered, until he augmented the warmth of the embrace by tucking her head beneath his chin. Roberta snuggled into him, slid her arms from his waist to around his back, and hugged him tight.

He was big and warm, and solid, and she'd never felt so cherished and loved in her whole life.

Loved? She pushed herself away. This was Garrett. Mr. Ranger. Molly's friend's poor brother who got stuck helping a pathetically distraught tagalong when he surely must have had dozens of better things to do.

"Aren't you supposed to be working today?"

The strange loss she felt when she pulled away from him was mirrored in Garrett's face for a few seconds, until he turned to pick up his guitar. "Yes, but I always take a little time off at sunrise Sunday morning to do this. The other guys respect that. They know I'll be back soon."

All she could do was nod.

"Well, I'd better be off." He didn't leave, but stood in front of her, holding the guitar in one hand.

Roberta nodded again, unable to stop staring as she processed what he said. The other rangers knew what he did and where he was going. He did this every Sunday, going through the trouble to make special arrangements, adjusting his work schedule. Sometimes, she barely had the courage to tell her co-workers she went to an organized church service on Sunday morning, when there was nothing else to do. She suddenly felt ashamed. This, too, would change. Roberta made up her mind. God caught her in her weakest moment and lifted her up when she'd pushed Him aside. She quickly counted the opportunities and blessings she didn't deserve. From now on, every Sunday, she would go to church to freely worship.

Garrett raised his free hand and brushed his fingertips along her cheek, then dropped his hand to his side. "See you later, Robbie."

He turned and left without a backward glance.

❧

The sky turned overcast, as predicted, but the rain managed to hold off, at least for the moment. However, Roberta estimated rain within an hour.

"Well," Molly mused as she tossed her sunscreen back into her bag. "I guess we don't have to worry about sunburn. Or towels. Or a blanket."

"I'm taking my towel anyway."

A knock on the door sounded. "Hey, in there!" Garrett's voice came loud and clear through the canvas walls. "You're not really going swimming, are you?"

Molly raised one finger to her mouth and pursed her lips, then called back to him through the closed door. "Who wants to know? You a cop?"

Roberta heard Garrett's soft chuckle, then he cleared his throat. He spoke in a deep clear voice. "Yeah. Park ranger. Official business. Open up in the name of the law."

Molly stifled a giggle, covering her mouth with her hand, then pointed to her pillow. "Come i–innnn," she called sweetly.

Garrett smiled, liking the sound of Molly's invitation. The second he opened the door, three pillows whapped him, sending him backward a step until he gained his bearings.

Before he could raise his arms to protect himself, another onslaught caught him.

"No fair!" he called out, lifting his hands and bowing his head to protect himself. "Resisting an officer! You're all under arrest!"

After a few more hits each, they stopped, and he raised his head to peek over his arms to see if it was safe. "What do you ladies think you're doing? Don't you think you're a little old to be having pillow fights?"

"Old!?"

"Oh, no. . ." He saw it coming in time to cover his head again. "Truce!" he called out from underneath his arms, wondering if they could hear him begging for mercy over their giggling. "I surrender!"

When he thought he was safe, he looked up. A quick glance at the three of them answered his earlier question. They were already changed into their bathing suits.

"I think my question's been answered. You're kidding, right?"

Gwen tapped her bare foot on the camper floor. "Does it look like we're kidding?"

He didn't bother to reply. In the remote chance of the weather changing, he had traded for beach duty for the afternoon. But, the weather hadn't cooperated, and it felt like the rain would start any minute. So often, campers did foolish things on their vacations, justifying it by saying they only had a few days' vacation and they were determined to do everything they planned, no matter what. He didn't expect his sister, of all people, to be like that.

Judging from her expression, and her arms folded across her chest, he wasn't about to argue. He shrugged his shoulders. "Suit yourselves. Just don't say I didn't warn you." Rather than fight a losing battle, he turned and left.

The rain set in while he made the rounds at the boating area. His patrol complete, he ran to the truck and drove to the beach, donning his bright yellow slicker before walking out into the pouring rain. As he expected, the beach was deserted, except for Molly, Roberta, and Gwen, splashing about in the lake. He stood on the shore, his arms crossed, not caring about the scowl he knew was on his face. Grinning like idiots, they waved at him. He raised one hand with a single wave back and recrossed his arms. They ignored his disdain and dove beneath the surface, all three of them in different directions. Witnessing enough, he headed back to the truck and back to the office. They'd be sorry, maybe not now, but they'd be sorry.

A rainy day provided a good opportunity to catch up on his paperwork. With a cup of coffee beside him at the desk, he drafted up the duty roster and scheduling for the following few weeks, made a few phone calls, ordered some supplies, and began to read all the reports that had piled up on his desk in the hot weather.

One report in particular caught his interest. It was a follow-up to his warning to the other rangers about the man prowling around who frightened Robbie.

Garrett sat back in the chair to study the other ranger's comments. The next night, Dean discovered a man trespassing in another campsite and issued a warning. The man had suspiciously checked out the next morning, and thankfully nothing had been found missing. Although it was impossible to be positive it was the same man without a confession, the timing and pattern were the same, and no more instances had been reported.

Garrett smiled as he signed the bottom of the page. Robbie would be happy to hear the situation was dealt with. Not that he wanted her to wander around alone at night in the campground, but he felt better about it.

He continued to read and initial more reports, then stopped when he picked up his own report concerning the eviction of the rowdy group containing the man who bothered Robbie in the water.

Garrett laid the paper on the desk and stared off into space. Despite the fact that she wasn't his type, he couldn't stop thinking about her. He probably should have been feeling sorry for her, but he didn't. True, she was devastated about her fiancé cheating on her. Who wouldn't be? The thing he personally valued the most in a relationship was trust, and he couldn't imagine a worse way to break that trust. His heart made a strange flip-flop in his chest as he remembered the series of events upon her arrival, how distraught she was. But instead of dwelling on it, she was dealing with it, and unlike so many people he'd seen facing a major upheaval in their lives, she was moving forward.

She was obviously a believer, and from what she'd told him, this Mike fellow wasn't. From the little she told him, Mike wasn't the right person to be her life's partner. Already, she had figured out she was better off without him, and he was strangely satisfied that she had.

They'd prayed for her to find that perfect partner God had in mind for her, but even though he'd prayed for it, he didn't like the idea that she would now go back to the dating scene. He wondered if he checked up on her periodically through Molly, if Robbie would mind. He almost laughed out loud. Robbie had made it more than obvious she wanted nothing to do with him, but if that were the case, why had he felt such a closeness when they worshipped and prayed together?

Garrett continued to stare into space. Just as he prayed for

Robbie to find the man God wanted for her, he often prayed for God to show him to that special someone. This morning, he hadn't. He no longer wanted to pray for it.

He let his gaze drift out the window, and he noticed the day had brightened. The rain had stopped.

He filed the last report away and checked his watch. If anyone was going to be stupid enough to use flammable liquids to try to light their campfires for supper, this was the time. Garrett gulped the last sip of his coffee, preparing himself to make the rounds to prevent anyone from blowing himself up for the sake of a roasted wiener.

But he knew where he was going first.

No noise emanated from the tent trailer as he approached it, making him wonder if they were still at the beach. He was about to turn around when he heard Molly's voice from within, whining.

"What I wouldn't give for my blow-dryer right now."

"Oh, Molly," Gwen whined back, "where's your sense of adventure?"

"I don't have a sense of adventure anymore."

Garrett smiled. He wasn't going to say "I told you so," but he could think it. He knocked. "It's me," he spoke into the door. "Can I come in?"

"Only if you have a battery-operated blow-dryer."

He opened the door anyway. Pale, with her teeth chattering, Robbie sat at the table, huddled with her sleeping bag around her, over her jacket, and long pants. Gwen stood beside the propane burner wrapped in her jacket, trying to warm her hands on the flame beneath the old aluminum coffee percolator as she waited for it to bubble, a towel wrapped snugly around her still wet hair. Her stiff posture and the jerky movements of her hands betrayed how uncomfortable she was. Molly sat awkwardly on one of the bunks, completely tucked inside her sleeping bag, only her head peeking out.

"Did you have a nice swim?" Garrett asked, fighting the urge to smile.

He couldn't help himself. He pressed his lips together tightly as they all glared at him. He knew this would happen. He and Gwen had done this before, when they were in their early teens. Against their parents' advice, they'd gone for a swim in the lake when it was raining, and then they had run all the way down the path in their bathing suits in the pouring rain to get back to the camper. For the rest of his life, he'd never forget that particular camping trip, and how cold they'd been that day. He hadn't stopped shivering until the next morning.

He had tried to tell them. They wouldn't listen. Roberta visibly shuddered, and all three of them looked up at him like frozen drowned little rats.

He felt his lower lip tremble, and he could no longer fight the corners of his mouth from tipping up. "Goodness, Gwen, you don't have as good a memory as I gave you credit for!" Unable to hold back any longer, Garrett burst out laughing. Three cold, wet bathing suits hit him in the face.

nine

Roberta nearly dropped her supper plate when Garrett stepped into the site. He wasn't wearing his uniform. All she recognized of his attire was the battered hiking boots. A light jacket blew open in the slight breeze, showing a sweatshirt with some kind of wild animal picture, accompanied by very worn jeans that fit him perfectly. The casual clothes made him appear even larger, if that were possible.

She nearly tripped over her own feet when she recognized the duffel bag he carried. Although she knew it was coming, she'd managed to push it to the back of her mind. She could no longer bury her head in the sand. He was off work now and here to join them on their camping vacation.

He casually tossed his belongings into the tent trailer, except for a cylindrical bag that Roberta recognized, which he leaned against the picnic table, then sat to join them, helping himself to a cup of coffee.

Molly craned her neck at the bag on the ground. "What's that?"

"My tent."

"Tent?" Molly stared at it like it was radioactive. "What do you mean, tent?"

"Tent. Portable sleeping accommodation."

"What's it for?"

"I'm going to sleep in it, Molly."

Roberta gulped. "No, Garrett. Please, don't feel you have to sleep outside again."

"I won't be outside. I'll be inside my tent. I'm not sleeping in there with you ladies." He jerked his thumb over his shoulder, and all three of them turned their heads, as if they'd never seen the tent trailer before.

She wondered if he would have slept inside the camper if she hadn't been there. She opened her mouth to speak, but Garrett cut her off.

"I know what you're thinking, Robbie. I would have slept in the tent anyway, even if you weren't here, so don't worry, okay?"

She clamped her mouth shut. Even though the sun came out and the ground was surprisingly dry, she still thought it would be cold and lumpy, but she was learning the hard way what it was like to try to change his mind, once it was made up.

"Hey, Bro, since you're here, if you want some food, you can have whatever's left over."

Garrett grinned as he walked back to the picnic table. Then Roberta nearly choked on her mouthful of barbecued pork chops at his sharp voice. "Hey! What's this?"

All three heads turned. Garrett held in his hand a battered mug containing a few wildflowers she'd picked earlier.

"I couldn't find anything else to use," Roberta mumbled, hoping she hadn't desecrated his favorite coffee mug by mistake.

"I didn't mean the mug. I meant these." He plucked the flowers out of the water and held them up for everyone to see.

"It *was* a flower arrangement."

"I beg your pardon?"

"You know, a flower arrangement. A centerpiece in keeping with the great outdoors."

"Where did you get these?" He held the flowers out towards her.

"I picked them from over there." Roberta pointed to the edge of the clearing, where a number of pretty wildflowers were growing.

"It's against the municipal bylaws to pick wildflowers."

Roberta cringed. "Oops. I didn't know."

Garrett dragged his palm down his face, then stared at her. "There's a sign right at the entrance to the park, next to the notice about the firewood. If every camper who came here picked just one flower, there would be no flowers left and the plants wouldn't come back the next year, and they'd be destroyed forever. I'm supposed to either report you, or issue you a warning."

Roberta stared at him, not caring that her mouth was hanging open. She didn't doubt that he would do it.

Molly's voice drifted from behind her. "You're off duty. You're out of uniform."

He didn't comment, but his stare told Roberta how seriously he took her infraction. However, even though it didn't seem like a big deal to pick a couple of small flowers, she could see his point. Like so many things in life that started small, if not checked properly, they would soon escalate. Like what happened in her Christian walk.

It had started with omitting saying grace when she went out because Mike said he felt awkward praying in public. That developed into missing church every once in a while, then more and more often. It had been such a gradual process that now, except for her recent talks with God since she'd come camping, she didn't remember the last time she'd prayed or even read her Bible. It started with one small thing, and if she had continued much longer, she wondered if there would have been anything left of her Christian lifestyle, just like the little wildflowers that could disappear forever, one small flower at a time.

"I'm sorry. I'll never do it again."

"It's okay; you didn't know." She watched as Garrett turned back to Gwen, completely unaware of the thoughts racing through her head. "Are you sure I can eat the rest of this potato salad? And the last pork chop?"

Fortunately, the incident was quickly forgotten as Garrett consumed the rest of the food, and by the time Roberta and Molly finished the dishes, the sun had completely set. Gwen had a cheerful fire going, and Garrett had set up a few tarps near the camper in case it rained again, as well as covering his small pup tent in the flat grassy area next to the tent trailer. He sat beside the fire, spearing a marshmallow onto a stick. Roberta purposely sat in the end chair of the row of four, which were placed neatly to the opposite side of the drifting plume of smoke. Gwen sat on the far end, and Molly sat between Roberta and Garrett.

"Oops, forgot my cup," Molly mumbled, and rose to disappear into the camper.

Grabbing the bag, Garrett smiled and shuffled one seat over to sit beside Roberta. He slowly waved the raw marshmallow on the end of the stick in front of her nose. "I'm an expert marshmallow roaster. Wanna share?"

"Uh, I don't think so," she mumbled.

He held the marshmallow close to the glowing embers, and turned to smile at her. "You don't know what you're missing." His shining smile made her breath catch. Roberta turned to study the fire.

Garrett didn't take the hint. He leaned closer, and whispered in her ear. "You'll make Gwen jealous. She's wanted to know my secret method for years."

Roberta turned to stare, but all he did was grin at her. Over his shoulder, she could see Gwen and Molly staring at the two of them. Her face warmed, but not from the heat of the fire.

As soon as he noticed her looking over his shoulder, Garrett's grin dropped. He pulled the half-roasted marshmallow out of the fire and turned to his sister. "Don't you two have something better to do?"

Gwen and Molly shook their heads and rested their chins in their palms, leaning forward. "No, not really."

He sighed loudly, then continued to roast the marshmallow in silence while Molly and Gwen chattered away. If Roberta didn't know any better, she'd think Garrett was coming on to her.

While Molly and Gwen chattered away, she supposed good manners dictated that she should talk to Garrett, since she would have to speak over him to join in their conversation.

Instead, she watched Garrett, which was a mistake, because he caught her looking. Without a word, he blew on the marshmallow to cool it and held the stick in front of her, offering it to her.

"I'm sorry; I don't really like marshmallows."

He smiled that killer smile she was beginning to know and love. "They're different roasted. Consider it changed, refined by fire, the impurities burned away, refined like silver, tested like gold, the end result being perfect and pure, just like Zechariah 13:9."

After a line like that, she couldn't help but accept the transformed marshmallow. And he was right. The rich creamy roasted texture melted in her mouth. It was delicious.

"Want to roast one yourself?"

"I don't think so. I've never roasted a marshmallow before, and I'd likely incinerate it."

He stabbed a new one onto the stick. "Here. I'll show you." He placed the stick in her hands, then covered both hands with one of his. With his other hand, he gently guided the stick to point the marshmallow to the side of the flames, near the glowing embers at the bottom of the fire. "Now we patiently wait."

Roberta waited, although not too patiently. She didn't know when it started, but Garrett's thumb trailed up and down her wrist, massaging gently, lulling her into a calm relaxation as they waited for the marshmallow to slowly brown.

"So, what do you think of camping?" his low voice murmured almost in her ear.

She turned her head to discover her face only inches from his. She froze, mesmerized. Their eyes locked, and she couldn't have looked away to save her life. In the flickering orange glowing light, his eyes shone with sincerity and seemed to gaze into her soul. "I like it," she mumbled.

"Good," he murmured.

Why did it seem like they weren't talking about camping anymore?

Slowly, he pulled her hands up but didn't break eye contact. "If you don't watch it, your marshmallow is going to burn."

Blinking rapidly, Roberta tried to regain her bearings. What in the world were they talking about? She stared at the golden brown marshmallow, steaming on the end of her stick. Gingerly, she touched it, then pinched it cautiously, pulled it off, and popped it into her mouth. It melted in her mouth just like the first one, except this time, she ate it slowly, savoring it, as if it were an expensive truffle from the downtown specialty chocolate store.

And he held eye contact the entire time.

This time, some of the molten marshmallow had dribbled onto her finger, so she stuck her forefinger into her mouth to suck it off. His gaze dropped to her mouth, and he watched. In a split second, she yanked her finger out of her mouth and wiped it on her jeans. *What just happened?*

Fortunately, neither Molly nor Gwen seemed to notice anything strange. She turned back to Garrett, but he simply smiled at her and stabbed another marshmallow onto his stick and started yakking away about some of their family's camping experiences. Roberta shook her head.

Garrett continued to talk. At first she was content to listen, but soon she began to answer his questions, and then gradually contributed more and more to the conversation until she found herself enjoying talking with him.

Before she knew it, it was after midnight. She knew sunrise came early, so they quickly packed things up and doused the fire.

She mumbled a quick good night to Garrett and followed Gwen and Molly into the tent trailer.

But she couldn't sleep. Before long, someone started snoring, which didn't help. She couldn't stop thinking about the exchange over the marshmallow. Why had it seemed so significant?

Earlier in the evening, the sky had clouded over again,

obliterating their view of the stars, making the night even darker. As she lay in her sleeping bag, it was so dark she couldn't tell if her eyes were open or not. She tried to count sheep to lull herself to sleep, when a shuffling noise came from outside. Her eyes shot open as she listened.

Then something fell off the picnic table.

She knew Garrett's tent lay only a few feet from the window of her side of the camper. Roberta unzipped the window.

"Garrett!" she whispered loudly through the screen. "Garrett! Did you hear that?"

A light came on inside his tent, and his head appeared in the opening.

He briefly shone the flashlight in the direction of the picnic table, then turned it off. "Go back to sleep; it's just a raccoon."

Roberta froze. A raccoon? She'd heard that line from him before. "That's what you said last time," she called out in a loud whisper. Whoever was snoring paused, snorted, then started up again.

The light in Garrett's pup tent went on again, she heard him unzip his sleeping bag, then a shuffle of clothing. He crawled out of the pup tent with the flashlight at his side, pointing to the ground, and stood beside her at the screened window. "Robbie, believe me," he whispered into the opening. "It's a raccoon."

A scraping sound drifted from beneath the picnic table.

"Garrett. . ." Roberta couldn't keep the waver out of her voice. "Do something!"

He chuckled softly, then aimed the flashlight beam to the noise. "Look."

From beneath the picnic table, animal eyes glowed from the reflection of the light. He aimed the beam directly at it. A raccoon huddled in the corner, eating bits of cereal that had spilled at breakfast time.

Roberta gasped. She'd never seen a live raccoon before, only on television. Aside from the fact that it was much bigger than she expected, the black mask around its eyes and the way it huddled under the table made it look like a cuddly little bandit. "It's so cute!" She looked toward the door, then started to wiggle out of her sleeping bag, when Garrett's open palm pressed on the screen.

He fired off his questions in rapid-fire succession, still managing to whisper. "Robbie! What are you doing? Where do you think you're going?"

"Uh, to see it. . ." she stammered, then glanced back and forth between his hand pressing against the screen and the path to the camper door.

"Don't let their adorable expressions deceive you. Raccoons are vicious. I hope you don't think you're going to walk up to it and pat it. When a raccoon feels threatened, it will attack. It's not a cute little puppy dog. It's a wild animal, very used to fighting for survival. Never forget that."

"Oh."

They watched it finish the rest of the cereal and waddle off in search of more treats left by other sloppy campers. Garrett's palm still lay pressed against the screen. Roberta was amazed at the size of his hand. Very lightly, she touched her fingertips to his, then trailed her hand down till the heel of her palm rested against his. His fingers extended a couple of inches beyond her own. She stared at their hands, touching, with the screen between. "Sorry to wake you for nothing. I've never seen a raccoon before."

Garrett's voice came out hoarse and croaky. "Then it wasn't for nothing." He dropped his hand, then backed up a step. "Good night, Robbie."

≈

At sunrise, armed with a handful of quarters, Roberta tiptoed past Gwen and Molly, who was still snoring, exited the camper, crept past Garrett's quiet tent, and headed to the amenities building to have a shower.

Upon her return nothing had changed, except the sunrise had brightened. The sun shone gaily in the blue sky above, promising another gorgeous day for camping. Rather than chance disturbing anyone, Roberta eyed the silent hammock. Did she dare?

She dared. She tiptoed into the camper, snagged her book, and returned to the hammock. Very carefully, she sat in it like Garrett showed her, leaned to the side, raised her feet, settled in, and lifted the book.

Approaching footsteps crunched in the gravel. "Hi. You're up early."

Not having read a word, she rested the book on her stomach. "Good morning, Garrett."

He stood beside the hammock and peered down at her. His duffel bag lay slung over one shoulder, and his wet hair evidenced that he, too, had snuck off for a shower. He also held a steaming mug in one hand. "So, did you dream about patting raccoons? Or feeding them, perchance?"

"No." What little sleep she did manage to get, she dreamed about him. Roberta inhaled deeply. Coffee. He had coffee. She wanted one, but she suspected he had been to the ranger camp to get it.

"I'm sorry, I didn't know you were up, or I would have brought you one, too. But I'll share."

She narrowed her eyes to stare at the steaming cup. After a gentle sip, he held the mug forward a few inches. It seemed a little too intimate to be sharing a morning coffee, so Roberta shook her head and raised her book. "That's okay, but thanks, anyway."

"Do you know what their plans are for today?" He jerked his head toward the camper.

She lowered the book back to her stomach. "No, but since the day looks so promising, I would think we'll go to the beach."

"Sounds like a good idea."

He didn't say anything, so she raised the book again.

"How long do you think they'll plan to sleep? The day's a-wastin'."

The book dropped back to her stomach. "I have no idea," she replied. "We were up at dawn yesterday." She acknowledged Garrett's nod. When he didn't comment further, Roberta lifted the book.

"Gwen usually gets up early camping," he said, glancing back to the camper, "but I don't know about Molly. What do you think?"

The book dropped. "Molly sleeps like a log. I have no idea." When he didn't comment further, she picked it up again.

"I don't know how you could sleep with all that snoring in there."

Roberta squeezed her eyes shut, thumped the book back down to her stomach, then stared up at him. He smiled back down. She hadn't slept well, but it hadn't been Molly's fault, it was his! "It didn't bother me," she said and lifted the book.

"Yes, the fresh air does that to a person. I always sleep better out here. Do you find that?"

She stared at the book, not seeing the print.

"Oh, are you trying to read? That's a good book. And watch out for Stanleigh; he's got something up his sleeve."

Roberta squeezed her eyes shut but kept the open book up in front of her. "Garrett!!"

Garrett chuckled softly as he walked away, speaking over his shoulder. "Enjoy your book, then, but you might be able to read it better if you turned it right side up."

She slammed it shut, groaned out loud, took aim, and threw it at him.

"Heads up!" he shouted as he projected its trajectory, and using his duffel bag like a baseball bat, he swung and deflected the book, sending it flying into the bush. He laughed out loud, making no effort to retrieve it.

Gwen stepped out of the camper. "What's going on out here? What time is it?"

Garrett stopped laughing but grinned ear to ear. "Better get that coffee going. I won't mention any names, but someone's crabby in the morning." He snickered and crawled into his pup tent.

ten

Having four people in such a small accommodation required careful placement of all utensils and personal goods. It took until lunchtime to get organized and decide on their afternoon activity, which would be another trip to the beach.

Roberta volunteered to put away the dishes after lunch. When she tucked the last plate away, she found Molly reading, Gwen talking to one of the other rangers on the road, and Garrett fast asleep in his hammock. She knew he'd put in many long days of working from sunrise to midnight, and they'd made him do all of the work taking the tarps down that morning. She felt sorry for him. She convinced the others to let him sleep while they went to the beach. As much as she enjoyed herself, Roberta couldn't get away from the feeling that something, or rather someone, was missing. She didn't want to miss him, but she did. Throughout the afternoon, she kept expecting him to show up. He didn't.

He hadn't moved by the time they returned. Gwen poked him.

He mumbled something unintelligible and covered his face with his forearm.

Gwen poked him again. "That's what I've always admired about you; you're bright and alert."

Only half coherent, Garrett mumbled his reply, but he couldn't make himself get up. In the background, he heard Robbie telling Gwen to leave him alone.

The sounds of activity slowly brought Garrett to complete wakefulness. He lay in the hammock, trying to figure out how he'd slept all day, which wasn't like him at all. Of course, it hadn't helped that despite being exhausted after a long stretch of working nearly round-the-clock, he'd tossed and turned all night thinking of Robbie.

His initial impression of her had made a complete turn-around. Compared to the state she was in when she first arrived, he could barely believe she was the same person, but over the space of a few short days, he'd personally witnessed the change. He realized now she'd had it in her all along.

He listened to her voice in the background, simply enjoying the sound of it. If he had to be honest with himself, he had to admit that he wanted to spend more time with her, even if she wasn't quite so receptive of him. The musical sound of her laugh made him smile even though he hadn't heard the joke, in addition to doing strange things to his heart.

He couldn't believe his own behavior last night. He'd never been one to try to romance a woman, if one could do such a thing beside a campfire, but if it hadn't been for his sister and Molly in the near vicinity, he would have kissed Robbie. As it was, he'd nearly kissed her anyway.

Not that he'd been sleeping, but when she called out to him when the raccoon scrounged through the campsite for food, the connection he felt when she touched his hand rocked him to his core. Was she the soul mate he'd been praying for? While he couldn't tell if she felt it too, he aimed to find out.

"Garrett, it's supper time, but if you expect to eat, you'd better be prepared to work for it after sleeping all day."

"No problem." He rolled out of the hammock and helped himself to a barbecued feast, ignoring Gwen as she nattered away at him over her opinion of him sleeping all afternoon.

He pretended to gripe when they told him to wash the dishes, not admitting he welcomed the chance to have something to do with his hands. He also wanted to watch Robbie from a distance. Strangely silent, Gwen dried the dishes, but left everything on the table for him to put away. He didn't mind.

Molly and Roberta made a fire, and he found all three women huddled around it after he had everything tidied up. He suggested they go for a hike to enjoy the evening, but they complained about being too tired. On the other hand, after sleeping all afternoon, Garrett was wideawake and raring to go.

It didn't take much convincing for him to haul another load of wood, nor did he protest when they cajoled him into cutting it all into smaller pieces, even though he knew it would burn faster that way.

He still had lots of energy. They complained he was making them more tired just watching him.

What he really wanted to do was go for a long hike up the mountain, but the sunset had already begun, and he knew the dangers of venturing outside the designated camping area after dark. He wasn't about to walk around the campground, he did that often enough when he was working.

When they all went to bed early, Garrett tidied up the campsite, fixed up his tent, and then watched the fire for a while. He couldn't believe it. He was bored.

Garrett stacked up the lawn chairs beneath the awning, doused the fire, and extinguished the lantern. He crawled into his tent and somehow managed to drift off to sleep.

❧

Roberta only half listened to Gwen and Molly's endless chatter the entire walk to the beach. Garrett walked alongside them, not saying a word, much to her disappointment.

Even though the day was already hot, the beach was nearly deserted, just like Gwen predicted.

As before, Molly and Gwen inched in, making faces as the cool water tortured them with every slow step. Roberta ran in, and Garrett ran at her side. He splashed in slightly ahead of her, diving in a split second before she did. Roberta rose out of the water, and as always, tilted her head back and swooshed her wet hair back off her face. When she opened her eyes, Garrett stood before her, his hair also slicked back, his body glistening in the sunlight. Tan lines on his upper arms drew her attention to his muscular forearms, which drew her attention to his physique in general. Although she'd already seen him without a shirt, she had to force herself not to gawk.

Roberta turned her head. This was Garrett. Mr. Ranger. Molly's friend's brother. Someone she'd never see again after this little camping vacation was over.

Molly and Gwen were in only up to their hips, gasping and flinching with every little step as they walked deeper.

Garrett met her gaze, grinned, and winked, making her aware that the ever-present dark sunglasses were missing. Roberta caught her breath and nodded back.

They dove in again, surfacing in front of Molly and Gwen. Garrett slapped the surface of the water with both hands, then laughed when they screamed. Roberta froze. She liked the sound of his laughter. Instead of joining in the splashing, she chose to watch as he splashed them again.

Molly shrieked. "No! No! Stop! Garrett, we're going to get kicked out! You'll get fired!"

"I'm not on duty, and no one here knows I'm supposed to know better." With that, he slapped the surface again, showering all four of them. "Besides, we're the only ones in the water. So who cares?"

Gwen splashed him back, which Roberta thought rather pointless, since he'd already been completely immersed twice, as had she. They couldn't possibly get any wetter.

Without warning, Garrett ducked under the surface, flipped Gwen up by her legs, then swam away, surfacing far away where she couldn't get him. When Gwen and Molly approached Roberta, suspecting her of some degree of involvement, Roberta sank beneath the surface and joined Garrett a distance away, begging him to save her. This time, it was a relief to only be kidding.

❧

As their vacation went on, Roberta relaxed more and more. And the more time she spent with Garrett, the more she enjoyed his company. In the mornings, they discussed and took a vote on the chosen feature activity of the day, and then they stayed together the entire time. Evenings they spent talking and joking around the campfire, enjoying the sunset and continuing the playful banter until bedtime.

On Wednesday, they awoke to an overcast sky. The odd raindrop had already begun to fall, so they scrambled to resurrect the tarps, then stood beneath them, dry if not warm, and watched it rain. For a while they played a board game Gwen found in one of the cupboards. Roberta even laughed when Garrett pretended to have difficulty choosing whether he wanted to be her partner or sit close beside her.

Because of the rain, they couldn't barbecue, and since it was Roberta's turn to cook, she did the best she could on the two propane burners inside the tent trailer. She had thought the close quarters all day, marooned in the small unit or in the lawn chairs beneath the tarp, would drive them all crazy, but they'd laughed and had a good time in spite of the weather.

She had to laugh when Garrett started the usual evening campfire huddled under an umbrella at the edge of the tarp. Amazed that no smoke drifted under the tarp, they sat close to the fire, welcoming the heat after a damp chilly day. After spending the entire day in the confines of the campsite, except for the occasional trip to the outhouse, they called it an early night. Roberta couldn't believe she'd enjoyed the day so much.

The sound of the rain on the camper roof lulled all four of them to sleep.

❧

"If I were at ranger camp, I'd be eating bacon and eggs."

Roberta noticed Garrett consumed every bit of cereal in his bowl and every drop of milk, despite his dissatisfaction.

Gwen crossed her arms and glowered at him. "If you want bacon and eggs, then you can cook breakfast. Don't expect me to go through all that work in the morning. I'm on vacation."

Molly's eyes opened wide. "Bacon and eggs. . .wow. . . Someone has to go grocery shopping this afternoon. If we buy bacon and eggs, you can cook, we'll all eat it, and then you can clean up the mess."

Garrett smiled. "I can handle that."

Molly enthusiastically created a shopping list filled equally with things they needed and didn't need. It took them all morning to agree on what they would eat every day as they made up the shopping list, and then they argued about who was going to go do the shopping. In the end, Roberta insisted that she would go later that afternoon, since she had not paid for a thing so far, and she had been there almost a week.

Roberta and Molly were elected to do the lunch dishes. Another ranger making the rounds stayed to talk to Garrett on the road, leaving the women alone at the picnic table as they worked. Molly tilted her head toward Garrett, then leaned to Roberta. Roberta leaned closer to hear Molly's whispered words. "So, what's going on between you and Garrett?"

Roberta flinched. She didn't know the answer herself. "Nothing," she mumbled.

"Could have fooled me," Molly whispered, glancing at Garrett as he laughed at something the other ranger said.

Roberta decided it would be a good time to study the scratches on the plastic plate as she dried it. "Nothing's going on," Roberta mumbled again.

"Don't think I haven't noticed the way he's been hanging around you."

Roberta had noticed herself. She had lost the ability to decide if it was good or bad. "He's just being friendly, I'm sure."

Molly snorted in a very unfeminine manner. "Just watch out. He's, like, really religious, you know."

Roberta paused, then wiped the plate with more force than necessary. In her opinion, the degree of Garrett's faith and conviction spoke volumes about his character and strengthened her opinion of him. But most of all, she wondered why Molly thought his faith would be a concern. Molly knew that she was a believer, even though she'd allowed Mike to draw her away from the church temporarily. She dearly wished Molly would make a decision to follow Jesus, but Molly remained passive, and it hurt. Knowing from experience that

Garrett held nothing of his faith back in his everyday life-style, Roberta wondered if Garrett's good example could make a difference to Molly.

"We've had a few good discussions, and I find his commitment refreshing."

"Oh." Molly mouthed the word more than actually said it.

Garrett jogged down the entranceway to stop beside them, thankfully halting their conversation. "A few of the guys are having a flag-football game, and they're short a few players. Are you ladies interested?" He paused as he looked down at Robbie, not needing to say how much shorter she was than everyone else. "If you want to be the cheering section, Robbie, we'll understand."

Roberta tightened her lips. A challenge had been issued. "I've got back pockets. I'll play."

"Are you sure about this?"

"If they need me to even up the sides, sure I'm sure." She'd played flag-football before. Once. When she was in grade seven. It was fun, as best she could remember.

Crossing the field on their way to the designated meeting place, a football flew toward them. Garrett jumped and caught it in one fluid motion and threw it back in a long even pass. Roberta wondered if perhaps she had been a little premature in her enthusiasm to join the game. Tennis was more her speed, especially when she considered the size of Garrett's ranger friends.

"Garrett's on my team!"

"You can have him; I want the redhead."

Molly blushed and giggled but didn't miss a step.

The man who called out received a series of elbows in his ribs but took it all in stride.

"I'm on his team." Molly continued to giggle.

Gwen and Molly exchanged winks. Roberta shuddered and opened her mouth to protest, but they beat her to the draw. Just her luck, they did need her to play to make the teams evenly numbered.

The tallest one of the bunch approached her and winked very obviously. "If you're on my team I won't care if we lose."

Roberta blushed. Before she could open her mouth to respond, Garrett stood beside her. His fingertips brushed her shoulder, and he stood so close she wondered if she could have slipped a piece of paper between them. "She's on my team," he stated bluntly. The man met Garrett's stare and backed away. Roberta wasn't quite sure she liked that, but she wasn't in a position to protest.

Everyone stuffed pieces of plastic, which suspiciously resembled pieces of a tarp, in their back pockets. They agreed on boundaries and started to play. She wondered about Garrett's decision to play football still wearing his sunglasses, but she decided not to question his judgment. She wondered if she'd recognize him in daylight hours if he didn't wear them.

Shorter and slower than everyone else, even Molly, Roberta still did her best. Her strength was catching, so unfortunately she became the recipient fairly often, and she quickly became winded being chased often, even though she didn't get very far.

During a much-needed break, they pumped some water from the well and splashed water on their faces, while a few of the men simply held their heads under the running water.

Refreshed, Roberta continued with renewed vigor. Despite her hesitations, she found herself enjoying the game and having a good time.

Roberta heard someone yell at her to receive a pass again. Running to catch it, she saw Gwen approaching at full speed out of the corner of her eye, meaning to intercept, with Garrett quickly catching up, since he was on her team.

In a hurry to catch it before Gwen, when Roberta jumped, she misjudged her distance. Her fingertips brushed the football in the air, and she started to fumble the ball. Desperately trying to catch it before it fell out of her hands completely, she forgot about Gwen. Just as she thought she had it, still in the middle of her jump, Gwen crashed into her with a thud.

Before she hit the ground, she heard Garrett mumble something, Gwen and Garrett grunted in unison, and the three of them fell to the ground together.

Instead of hitting the ground, she heard as well as felt the rush of air as she landed on top of Garrett. Gwen bounced off to the side, rolling in the grass until she came to a stop melodramatically on her stomach, arms and legs splayed. Having overdone it so badly, no one gave her any sympathy but laughed instead.

Although her landing was softer than Gwen's, Roberta wished she would have landed on the grass, because now she had to get off of Garrett with her dignity intact.

She scrambled to her feet. "Oops, sorry," she mumbled, as she backed up a step. Something crunched under her foot, twisting her ankle. Still feeling shaky from her recent mishap, she couldn't regain her balance soon enough. Rather than make it worse, she simply let herself fall, landing with a thump in a sitting position with her legs sprawled out.

She sat inelegantly on the ground beside Gwen, who was lying face down on the ground, and Garrett, who was lying face up, as everyone else came running to check for casualties.

Before she checked in the grass to see what she'd tripped on, she registered that Garrett wasn't wearing his sunglasses.

Roberta felt sick.

She didn't want to look, but she had to.

Beside her foot lay the remains of Garrett's sunglasses. Before he got to them first, Roberta grabbed them. One arm stuck out at a horrible angle. She wiggled it just a little, and it snapped off completely. With one piece in each hand, she whipped them behind her back.

Garrett rose to his feet and stared at her. He didn't say a word.

Roberta gulped, tried to smile, and failed miserably. "You don't want to see them. It will be less painful that way."

He didn't comment.

Roberta scrambled to her feet, still holding the pieces

behind her back. "I'm going to go into town now to pick up the groceries. If you come with me, I'll buy you a new pair. I'm really sorry."

After a charged silence, Garrett sighed. "No, I probably shouldn't have been wearing them. It's not your fault. Don't worry about it."

"I mean it, Garrett. Please? For me?"

She gave him her best puppy-dog look as he hovered above her. She could see the indecision on his face, but finally his features softened, and he nodded. "Okay. I don't have a spare pair, so I guess I don't have much choice."

"Well, if we're going to be back in time for supper, we had better leave now. Molly, can I borrow your keys?"

❧

Garrett drew in a deep breath, releasing it slowly. He must have been delusional to invite her to play football with the guys. In what was planned as a noncontact game, this could only happen to Robbie. For such a little thing, she'd sure packed quite a wallop. She'd knocked the wind right out of him.

Molly searched her pockets for her keys. He couldn't believe Molly would so freely offer her car to Robbie. The woman couldn't even run in a straight line. Garrett valued his life too much. "I'll drive."

He walked away before anyone could protest.

eleven

A beat-up looking jeep of some kind inched into the campsite. Roberta almost told the driver he was in the wrong campsite when her breath caught. The driver was Garrett.

"Hop in."

The immaculate interior contrasted radically with the exterior, which had apparently seen more than a few mountain adventures.

"Like it?" He grinned.

Roberta ran her hand along the plush seat, and then her gaze drifted to a large dent on the hood of the vehicle. "This thing looks like you drove it over a cliff or something."

Garrett's smile faded. "It's been rolled a couple of times when I was off-roading, but I'm quite a safe driver. I never take unnecessary chances."

Roberta hadn't meant to question his driving ability. She rested one hand on his forearm, then almost forgot what she was going to say at the odd squishy feel of the hair under her palm. She yanked her hand back, and he stared down at his arm, as if she'd left some foreign substance on his skin.

"That's not what I meant," she stammered. "I trust you. And we'd better get going. I'm sure you're going into serious withdrawal without your sunglasses."

Saying it out loud made her realize that she did trust him, not merely that he wouldn't do something foolish and get them killed on the road, but really trusted him. For anything.

Upon their arrival at the mall, Roberta led him to her favorite department store and straight to the sunglasses. Within seconds, she spotted the perfect pair, almost identical to the ones that she broke.

"Here, try these."

He put them on without looking in the mirror, wiggled them, then nodded. "Yeah, they feel fine."

"Aren't you even going to look at yourself?"

He shrugged his shoulders, removed them from his face, and read the tag. "What for? They fit right, they're a good quality name brand, and they offer a good level of UV protection."

"Don't you want to know what you look like in them?"

He slipped them back on and scrunched up his cheeks as if feeling them on his face, which raised the glasses up along the bridge of his nose, then let them drop. "No."

Roberta couldn't believe her eyes. She found it difficult to believe that he could be so handsome in sunglasses when he hadn't even bothered to see how they looked on him.

He took them off and started to walk toward the cashier when Roberta stopped him.

"Hold on a sec," she said. "Let me see those."

He handed them to her without thinking. Roberta turned and proceeded to the cashier.

"Robbie? Where are you going?"

"I'm going to pay for them. I broke your other ones, so I'm going to pay for your new ones."

"You don't have to do that." He held out his hand to take them back, but she didn't cooperate.

"I broke them; I replace them."

Since she was unemployed, Roberta cringed at the price, but knowing he worked outside all day, every day, he needed to have good quality sunglasses. She suspected the ones she broke were equally as costly.

While waiting for him to unlock the car door, she removed the price tag. He opened the door and held it for her, but instead of settling in, she handed him the new sunglasses. "You'd better take them now, before I sit on them or something."

After thanking her politely, he slid them on, nodded, and walked around to the driver's side.

"Do you mind if we make a quick stop at my place? I think I should check on my plant and take in my mail. It's not far from here," she said.

"Not at all. Which way?"

She directed them to her small rented duplex.

It felt strange to be back. Although nothing had changed, she remembered the state she'd been in when she left. Even though it had been only a week, she felt like she'd made up for a year's worth of maturing in the short space of time. She stood in the middle of the living room, staring, feeling oddly out of place.

❧

Garrett followed her inside, closing the door behind him. He left his brand-new sunglasses on the coffee table as he checked the place out. The furniture, while sparse, was well-chosen, comfortable, and well-matched. "Nice place." He honestly liked it. It suited her. Clean, neat, practical. "You live alone, right?"

"Yes, I do. Is it that obvious?"

"You have one couch, one painting, and everything you have matches everything else."

She smiled in reply, warming his insides.

He followed her into the kitchen, where a large plant sat in the sink. She flooded it with water and waited for it to drain.

"It's my only living houseplant. I left on such short notice and I didn't have anyone to ask to house-sit, so I left it in the sink in a puddle of water and hoped for the best. Looks like it's going to live." She felt the leaves and gave it a pat.

While she fussed with her plant, a rainbow reflection caught Garrett's attention. Expecting to see a prism hanging by the window, he followed the path of the light. Not seeing one, he continued to follow where it would have reflected from, his next guess being some kind of crystal ornament that women liked so much. Then he saw it, but it wasn't what he expected. His stomach clenched when he discovered an engagement ring in the middle of her kitchen table.

He whistled between his teeth, holding it up and turning it

as it caught the light. "What a rock," he mumbled. Even though he'd never priced engagement rings, any fool could see this one cost a small fortune. He would never be able to afford a ring like this as a park ranger, even after he graduated.

Robbie sighed and shrugged her shoulders. "Yes, it's very expensive. I know people who drive cars worth less than that ring. I didn't pick it out, but I did have it appraised for insurance purposes, and I couldn't believe the value."

After a comment like that, he didn't feel right holding it. Another man's ring. Given to Robbie. He laid it quickly on the table, as if it would burn him if he touched it any longer.

Roberta picked it up, tossed it in the air, caught it, then threw it carelessly onto the counter. Garrett cringed when it landed, tinkling as it slid until it hit the tile wall, and stopped.

He'd almost expected her to get all teary-eyed again, but instead, she looked him straight in the eye, then stared off into space. "You know, Garrett, for all the money spent on that gorgeous ring, it's worth nothing to me. All it represents is a hollow promise that's been broken into a million worthless pieces. To be given a ring a fraction of that value with a sincere commitment of love and trust and loyalty would be worth far more than all the gold and diamonds in the world."

He didn't answer. What could he say?

Robbie ran her fingers through her hair, stared at her open palm, then grimaced. "I'd feel awkward saying this to anyone else except you, but I think you've already seen me at my worst. I need a real shower, not the quarter-a-minute kind. Would you mind if I basked in the luxury of my own shower while we're here? I think I have some magazines or something if you want to read. I promise to hurry."

"No rush. Your couch looks softer than those wooden picnic benches, so I'll just take it easy for a while."

To prove his point, he sauntered into the living room, lazed back on the couch, and linked his fingers behind his head. "Take your time. Wake me up when you're done." He winked as she appeared in the doorway between the kitchen and the living room.

Roberta had never wanted nor appreciated her own shower so much in her life. She nearly ran to her bedroom to select clean clothes and laid them out on her bed before locking herself in the bathroom. She'd also never fully appreciated the adjoining door from the bathroom to the bedroom. She dumped her dirty clothes in the hamper, and turned the water on extrahot, without needing a pile of extra quarters nearby.

The shower was always a place of quiet contemplation. Despite the heartache of a week ago, and though it had been a rough ride, she thanked God for the final result. And God was faithful through it all, even though she hadn't been. She'd pushed God aside and ignored Him when she thought she was pursuing her own happiness. God knew better. God knew Mike and what would have been in store for her had she stuck with him. Even though she wasn't very grateful at the time, she now appreciated seeing Mike's true colors. It had hurt like a slap in the face, but at least she could do something about it before it was too late.

Then, when she'd felt all but deserted, God put Garrett in her path. He'd taught her a lot about herself, and for that she'd always be grateful. She'd have to do something special for him before their holiday ended, because she'd likely never see him again. The realization made her strangely sad.

Having the burden of Mike's betrayal lifted almost made her sing the last song she'd sung with Garrett at the lakeside, a song of reverence and respect for God's enduring love. However, her singing, especially in the shower, was far from professional caliber. God wouldn't mind, but she thought Garrett might. In fact, if she started singing unaccompanied, knowing the way Garrett so readily appeared to help her when he thought she needed it, he would probably think she was in pain and break down the bathroom door and embarrass them both. She'd embarrassed herself in front of him enough in the past week to last a lifetime.

She had just turned off the water when she heard the door-bell. She scrambled out of the shower to grab her towel and hurry through the door to her bedroom when she heard the creak of the front door opening. Instantly she relaxed, grateful not to have to hurry. Whoever it was, Garrett could either tell them to make themselves comfortable, or if it was a sales-man, send him away.

Her hand froze on the towel bar when she heard an angry voice.

"Where's Robbie?"

Mike. She sucked in a deep breath and yanked the towel down.

Garrett answered, pointedly polite. "My name's Garrett. And you must be Mike."

"Yeah, Garrett," he sneered, spitting out Garrett's name. "What are you doing here? Where's Robbie?"

Garrett used the same overly pleasant tone as when someone argued with him while on duty as park ranger. "She's busy, and I'm waiting for her. Can I help you with something?"

Roberta didn't bother with her dripping hair. She frantically tried to dry herself as quickly as possible, scurrying to her bed to collect her clothes.

"I need to talk to her. I want to make a deal."

She didn't like the sound of Mike's voice, an irritated tone she'd heard only once, when he was very, very angry. She'd never been so grateful for Garrett's presence, although she certainly didn't want to get him involved in her personal problems any more than he already was.

Garrett replied, overly pleasant again, but firm. "I don't think she wants to talk to you."

"That's too bad. I'm going to talk to her, whether she wants to hear it or not."

"Well, Mike, I beg to differ. I think you should go. By the way, friend, have you been drinking? Or anything else that we don't want to talk about?"

"Look, pal, that's none of your business. And where has

Robbie been for the past week? With you?"

Garrett's voice lost its pleasant edge. "I don't think that's any of *your* business."

The conversation seemed to be getting too heated in there. Roberta wanted Mike gone, and she wanted him gone *now.* She tried to slip on her underthings.

"I'm her fiancé. I make it my business."

Roberta stood on one leg, trying to force one damp foot through the leg opening of her shorts and nearly fell on the floor at Mike's words. As usual, he made it his business when he wanted something. The selfish creep. She bounced on the bed, then shoved both feet in while sitting and stood to fumble with the zipper.

Garrett's voice dropped to a low even pitch. "You're not her fiancé anymore."

Mike made a choked laughing sound, not that it sounded like he thought Garrett's reply was funny. "Well, well. Surprise, surprise. And how long has this been going on? Are you the reason she's been holding back on me? Hmm, Garrett?"

Roberta's hand froze, and she managed to yank the zipper up with a jerk, nearly catching her fingers. Couldn't he understand that she wouldn't sleep with Garrett because she had *morals,* something Mike obviously knew nothing about.

"That's enough. Let me show you to the door."

"I'm not leaving without my ring!" Mike shouted.

"You're leaving. Now."

She couldn't believe the angry sound of Garrett's voice, and she couldn't believe Mike wasn't long gone. Robbie pulled her T-shirt over her head, soaking the neck opening with her dripping hair, then nearly choking herself as it got stuck.

"If she's ready to play by my rules, then I'll think about giving her her job back."

"Why you. . . She'd never. . ."

Roberta nearly lost her lunch. She tried to ram her hand through the sleeve opening and missed. She didn't need or want her job back, and she wanted Mike out of her house and out of her life forever. How could she have thought she loved this man? How could she have ever considered marrying him?

She needed to put a stop to the ugly scene in the living room. Fully dressed at last, she started for the bedroom door just as she heard the sickening thud of a fist finding its mark. She couldn't tell who hit whom. Although Mike deserved it, she couldn't see Garrett throwing the first punch.

She ran down the hall in bare feet, and she heard cursing as Mike hit the sidewalk, a rustling of her bushes, hopefully the rosebush, followed by the slam of her front door.

"What's going on in here?" she called frantically as she skidded to a halt. Garrett stood, his back to her, leaning with his palms pressed at shoulder height against the door.

"Garrett! Say something!"

"You had a visitor."

She waited.

Slowly, he turned to face her with a slightly crooked smile. "He's gone now." One eye was already starting to swell shut.

Roberta covered her mouth with her hands. "Oh, Garrett!" she gasped.

He winced at the same time as he grinned.

"Oh, Garrett, I'm so sorry! Does it hurt?"

"Am I expected to be brave or truthful?"

Roberta cringed. Turning toward the kitchen, she called over her shoulder as she started to run, "Let me get you some ice. Sit down."

Instead of sitting, he followed her into the kitchen. She guided him to one of the chairs before she dumped some ice into a plastic bag, then covered it with a clean dish towel and gently pressed it to his eye.

When he flinched at the contact, Roberta nearly cried. Determined to be strong, she bit her quivering bottom lip and twined the fingers of her other hand through the hair at the back of his head to steady it, maintaining contact with the compress.

He raised his hand to push it away, but she shook her head.

"It's not that bad, really," he complained.

"Quit trying to be valiant. I know Mike works out at the gym." Garrett flinched again when she moved it to cover his whole eye. "Don't move," she whispered hoarsely.

Obeying her command, he stiffened, not moving a muscle, until she removed the cloth to reshape it as the ice melted.

"Am I all better?"

"Hush," she choked out, still trying to assimilate what she'd heard. Mike had let her know in no uncertain terms what he thought when she turned him down, but he had never resorted to violence or threats in the past. But from the brutality present in his voice, she didn't care to take that chance. Date rape really happened, and she had no intention of becoming another statistic.

She removed the compress to shuffle the ice in the bag. Before she had the opportunity to reapply it, Garrett's hand grasped her wrist.

"It's okay, Robbie, I don't think any more ice would make a difference. What's done is done."

"I'm so sorry; it's all my fault."

He gave her such a sad smile she had to bite her bottom lip to stop it from quivering. "I should have seen it coming. Now forget about it. We'd better go get those groceries, or else we'll have to face the wrath of two very hungry campers if we're late with their supper."

All she could do was nod.

On their way out the door, Garrett picked up his sunglasses off the table and very gingerly placed them on his face. She couldn't help but stare. The large sunglasses managed to hide almost all the swelling, but she could see some discoloration already starting below the lower part of the frame.

For the first time since they were alone together, Garrett remained silent. Overcome with guilt over everything that had happened to him because of her, before Roberta realized what she was doing, she found herself doing what Garrett had done up till now. Chattering. Endlessly. She talked about her neighborhood as they drove away, her family, her perception of her camping experience so far, making him smile when she openly admitted how out of her league she was when she first arrived and how much she'd learned so far. She asked him questions about his studies, his future career plans, and about what in the world a wildlife biologist would do, especially in the winter when there weren't any campers to harass.

He outright laughed at that, doing strange things to her insides.

Garrett never removed the sunglasses the entire time they shopped. Quickly filling their list, Roberta insisted on paying as Garrett packed. Instead of picking something to cook for supper, Roberta bought a bucket of chicken as a treat.

ea.

As expected, by the time they arrived back at the campsite, Molly and Gwen pounced upon them, complaining bitterly about starvation until they saw what they'd brought.

They hadn't been missed. Molly and Gwen described their day of searching the campground for the group of rangers they'd played football with. Disappointed at not being able to find them, Molly and Gwen gave up and went to the beach and had been pleasantly surprised to find them there, not on duty. They'd had a wonderful time.

Garrett remained in the background as the women ate, listening to them chattering away. Fortunately, no one paid attention to him. On the drive back, when Robbie wasn't looking, he'd snuck a peek at his eye in the rearview mirror, and it looked worse than it felt, if that was possible. Almost swollen shut, every time he blinked, the mere contact of his upper and lower eyelids against each other created such pressure that he saw stars all over again. He'd developed a pounding headache all through the left side of his face, and even though it left him with no depth perception, he kept his left eye shut. With the sunglasses on, hopefully no one would notice.

Not wanting to cause a scene or embarrass Robbie, he slunk into the hammock once he finished his supper, where no one would pay any attention to him.

He made no effort to help them build their campfire or light the lantern as sunset approached. He linked his fingers behind his head and crossed his ankles in the hammock, pretending to be asleep. He'd never had a black eye before, and he wondered how long it would throb like this, making him also wonder if he'd be able to sleep tonight. The day changed into nightfall, and still he stayed in the hammock, silent. With darkness came the chill of the night air, but he didn't want to leave the haven of his hammock. He'd have to take off his sunglasses sooner or later, and although he knew it was unrealistic, he thought if he waited long enough, maybe they wouldn't notice.

Knowing they wouldn't ignore him forever, he was still caught off guard when Gwen called him. "Wake up, Garrett, or you won't be able to sleep tonight."

He didn't answer, hoping she'd leave him alone, and that no one would notice the hammock trembling because he was shivering. He mentally kicked himself for not changing into long pants when he had the chance. Or at least changing into something with long sleeves.

"Garrett!" Gwen called, this time from above him. He looked up at her and grinned, hoping that she couldn't see his face in the dark shadow of the hammock. "Are you sick or something? You didn't eat any marshmallows. I didn't know there were so many in one bag."

"Oh, I must have fallen asleep," he mumbled.

"Are you still wearing those things after dark? Are you nuts? And let me see them. These are the new ones Robbie got you, right?" Before he realized what she was doing, Gwen reached down and pulled the sunglasses off his face. He couldn't protest without causing a scene, so he painted a grin on his face, hoping she wouldn't look at him. He'd managed to hide his face all evening, first with the sunglasses and then under cover of darkness. If his face remained enough in the shadow of the hammock, their secret would be safe for a while longer.

"Aren't you cold? I've got a jacket on and I'm by the fire. Are you avoiding us for some reason?"

He was. But he wouldn't admit it, especially to his sister.

"If you don't get out of there, I'm going to dump you."

He didn't need this attention. "You'd better not."

Without warning, she grabbed one side of the hammock and lifted it up. Caught off guard, his arms shot out to the sides in a reflex action, and he grabbed the edges of the hammock to keep from falling out. Gwen let it go, causing it to rock back and forth violently. His head pounded from the sudden movement, and it felt like something stabbed him in the eye. Completely forgetting himself, he sat up with a jolt. "Knock it off, Gwen!"

She never replied. Her eyes opened wider than he'd ever seen. She gasped and leaned closer to him. "What happened to you?"

Three pairs of eyes glared at his face. Robbie visibly paled, her mouth opened, but no sound came out. He bared his teeth in what was probably the phoniest smile of his life, the mere movement making his face hurt. Mustering his dignity, he rose from the hammock and seated himself at the empty lawn chair by the fire.

"Would you believe me if I said I had an accident with a big tree?"

No one spoke. Gwen shook her head.

"I had a disagreement with Smokey the Bear?"

Robbie broke the silence. "It's my fault," she squeaked out in a tiny little voice.

Garrett cringed as she continued.

"Garrett and Mike had a bit of an altercation."

Molly gasped. "Mike? When did you see Mike?"

"He kind of showed up when we stopped by my house."

Molly's eyes opened wider, if it was possible. "You had a fight? A fistfight? You?"

Garrett couldn't help himself. He smiled, despite the movement it made to his face. "It wasn't exactly a fistfight, Molly." After the shock of Mike plowing him in the face, he'd been so angry, that he'd picked Mike up by the scruff of his neck and, exhibiting great restraint, threw Mike, flailing arms and legs and all, outside into the bushes before slamming the door. He didn't know how he hadn't hit Mike back, but after the fact, he was grateful for the grace God gave him not to lower himself to Mike's level.

Molly walked to him, leaning forward to get a better look at his face. "Well, I hope you flattened the little creep!"

"Molly!!!" Robbie gasped as she ran to his side.

Garrett grinned. "We'll just say I escorted him out the front door against his will."

He raised his hands to the fire, leaning forward to warm himself, signaling his wish to change the subject. As always, Gwen knew he had no intention of discussing it, and she led the conversation into tall tales and bad jokes.

Midnight came quickly. Garrett crawled into his pup tent and the women retired into the camper for the night.

twelve

Any other day, Garrett thought the fussing would have amused him. He might even have appreciated being spoiled. Not today. The swelling had subsided enough to not be painful, but he knew it was still ugly. But worse than the women hovering, he knew the other rangers would bug him, and he didn't want to explain how it happened. And he could only wear the sunglasses until sunset.

"Would you like another cookie? Or more coffee?"

If he had any more coffee he'd burst his bladder. "No, thanks, Robbie. But I know what I would like. Why don't we all do something away from the campsite? I have to go back to work this afternoon, so this is my last chance at any time off. By midafternoon, the weekend campers will begin to arrive, and I'll be due back on duty."

Molly groaned. "Don't you want to relax? You walk around all the time."

"It's different when I have a routine to follow. Who wants to check out the waterfall?"

Robbie perked up. "Waterfall?"

"Yeah." Garrett pointed north to the trail leading up the mountain. Robbie's head turned to follow the direction of his finger. "At an average pace, it takes about an hour to reach it. If anyone here can handle it."

Gwen and Molly shot him a dirty look. He knew they didn't like to walk in the wilderness, and even if they did, it wasn't them he wanted to walk with. Garrett smirked beneath his sunglasses.

"I'd rather play football," Molly grumbled.

He gritted his teeth, then smiled at Robbie. "I'll bet it'd make a great picture."

"Picture?" Robbie turned her head to the direction of the camper, where her camera sat in the middle of the table. Up till now he'd managed to stay clear of her with that thing, but some things were worth the sacrifice.

He waited, almost able to see the gears whirring inside her head as she considered it. "Okay!" she chirped. "I just have to change. I'll be right back!" She ran inside the camper, and all the curtains pulled shut.

"Garrett, I have to make a trip to the little girl's room. Care to come for a walk with me?" Judging from Gwen's stone face and less-than-discreet glances to the road, he didn't think he was going to like what she intended to say. But all that coffee, graciously delivered, had taken its toll.

Gwen remained silent until they were well out of earshot of the campsite. He didn't know why. If this one was like any other of their normal conversations, no one would be able to follow it, anyway.

"Don't think I don't know what's happening, Garrett."

He hated these conversations. Garrett sighed loudly. "Why don't you tell me all about it?"

"This is different. Tell me what's going on."

Garrett nearly stumbled. No matter how much time they'd ever spent apart, he'd never had to explain himself to his sister. Never. "I don't know if I can."

"You're falling in love with Robbie, aren't you?"

He walked slowly in step with Gwen. "Does it show?"

"It does to me." They stopped in front of the path to the outhouses, but Gwen remained on the main road with him.

Garrett shoved his hands into his pockets and stared at the ground. He'd never been lost for words with his sister before and found it difficult to explain what was happening in his head. He thought about it for a minute, then lifted his head and faced her. "She's different than anyone I've ever met. I know she's not really my type, but there's something about her that makes me feel complete, like the last piece of a puzzle fitting into place."

Gwen nodded. "I was afraid of that."

"Oh? How so?"

Gwen laid her hand on his shoulder, and he didn't think this was a good sign. "Has it occurred to you that she might not feel the same way?"

"Don't be ridiculous, Gwen. All I need to do is talk to her."

"I don't think so this time, Bro."

"I've prayed about it, and God's answered me. I know it."

Gwen shook her head. "All I can say is, don't get your hopes up. Sometimes these things can be one-sided. You know I'll pray for you, but I don't want you to be disappointed."

He shook his head, but he didn't say anything. All he had to do was talk to her.

They returned to the campsite in silence, where Robbie waited for him dressed in a stark white T-shirt, a pair of cream-colored sweatpants, and her white sneakers, which weren't as white as they used to be. He tried to smile as she fiddled with the camera slung around her neck.

"See you later," Robbie called as Gwen joined Molly.

Garrett could see Molly looking around, trying to be discreet, which was a first for Molly. After his conversation with his sister, he strained to hear what they were saying.

Molly leaned to Gwen. "He's got it bad, doesn't he?" she said in a stage whisper he couldn't help but overhear.

Gwen nodded. "Yup."

"She doesn't, does she?"

"Nope."

"This could be interesting."

"Yup."

That was okay. Garrett knew that this time, his sister was wrong.

≥∘

Roberta walked beside Garrett as they wandered along the mulch pathway of the nature trail. For the first time, Garrett didn't fill every minute yakking about the squirrels, birds, trees, bushes, clouds, weather, or anything else that crossed his mind. At first she enjoyed the peace and quiet, listening to the soft crunching of their footsteps on the path, the birds chirping, and the chattering of the odd squirrel without an explanation on the species or genus or a description of their habitat. Finally, though, she couldn't stand it any longer.

She opened her mouth to ask if something was wrong, but as she did, she heard water trickling and splashing in the distance. "Listen! We're close to the waterfall! I can hear it!"

"Yes," Garrett replied softly. The low timbre of his beautiful baritone voice almost made her lose her step. "A few more minutes, and we'll be able to see it."

The volume of the moving water increased as they continued, until finally she could see it.

The water cascaded over the edge of a small cliff, bouncing and splashing on smooth, shiny black rocks below. The entire scene glittered in the sunlight, creating a small shimmering rainbow to the right above the stream. The brightness of the water contrasted magnificently with the dark bushes surrounding it, creating a natural frame, showing off the elegant beauty of the flowing water as nothing else could.

She lifted her camera.

Garrett stood back quickly.

After snapping a few pictures, she lowered it and let it hang freely about her neck. She watched his head lower almost imperceptibly, as if analyzing the status of the camera. Roberta sucked her lower lip, wondering if she should ask. Encouraged by his silence, she did. "Can I take your picture by the waterfall?"

He stiffened, and his lips tightened. She couldn't tell where he was looking behind the sunglasses. "I won't smile."

She tried to bite back a nervous laugh. "I didn't expect you to, although your smile must do your dentist proud. Besides, with that hat and your sunglasses constantly covering your face, a smile would seem out of character. All you need to complete the image is a big cigar and a submachine gun."

His mouth opened as if he was going to say something, but then he stopped and smiled. In a flash, Roberta raised the camera to one eye and clicked without taking the time to focus, hoping for the best, then lowering it just as quickly. "Why do you hate having your picture taken?"

The smile faded, making her sorry she had asked. She waited, unsure if he would tell her the reason or tell her to mind her own business. He stared off into the waterfall and rammed his hands in his pockets. She joined him at his side.

"You know Gwen and I are twins?"

"Yes."

"Well, when we were little, my dad lost his job. To make some money, my mom took us to audition for magazine ads and the like, having cute little twins pose, and one agency signed a contract with us." He stared into the water, bent to pick up a rock, and threw it in. "I remember, a long time after we started, I finally saw some of the pictures. I'll never forget how awful they were or how it felt to look like that."

"Oh, come on. I'll bet you were a cute kid."

"I wasn't. At a certain age, Gwen and I looked almost exactly alike. Instead of cutsie twin pictures, the photographers tried an experiment, and it worked, at least from a commercial standpoint. For one particular ad sequence, they made her up and posed her as the cute little girl she was, and dressed and made me up to be the identical doofus little boy. The ads were a success, so they kept on with the same theme. I was completely humiliated, yet I knew it was important to my parents, although at the time I didn't know why, so I did my best and stuck with it, but I wouldn't wish that on any kid."

He cleared his throat and picked up another a rock. "My mother honestly thought people laughed because they thought we were cute, but the truth was that the contrast between the perfect little girl and the pitiable little boy made me feel pathetic."

Roberta didn't know what to say, but the sight of a grown

man fighting unpleasant childhood memories tore at her heartstrings. "I'm sure no one meant it personally."

"Well, I was just a kid, and I took it personally. And I still can't get over my hatred of cameras. As if you couldn't tell." He turned his head, and she thought he was looking at her, but she couldn't tell for sure. "I make myself scarce when the camera comes out at family functions, too."

Roberta wished she could say something to ease things, but her mind was blank, so she said a silent prayer for peace of mind for him. They watched the waterfall, standing side by side.

"So, do you have any plans for when you get home from camping?"

Roberta wasn't sure what he meant. "Not really, except for trying to find another job, but I don't think I'll have any problems. I've got a steady work history and a good letter of recommendation. I guess today is the end of any time off for the rest of the summer for you. Then you're going back to college in the fall, right?"

"Yes." He stuck his hands back in his pockets. "Do you think Mike will bother you again? If you need any help keeping him away. . ." His voice trailed off, becoming drowned out by the steady drone of the waterfall.

"I don't think he'll be a problem. You already showed him he was less than welcome."

Conversation lagged. Garrett inched closer, then grasped both her hands in his. "Can I ask you a personal question, Robbie?"

She wasn't sure she wanted to hear his question, but she couldn't imagine things getting much more personal than anything she hadn't already told him or his confession of why he hated cameras. She doubted his parents knew how he felt, and although she suspected there were few, if any, secrets between him and Gwen, she didn't think even Gwen knew this. So Roberta nodded.

"Why did you say you'd marry him? Were you in love with

him, I mean, *really* in love?"

So she was wrong. Things could get much more personal. Roberta wondered if she could avoid the question, but he held her hands just firmly enough that she couldn't pull away without looking churlish after he'd bared his soul. As she answered, she could see her own reflection in his sunglasses looking back at her. "At the time, I thought I was, but now, looking back, it was more familiarity. We were always together, every day all day at work over the space of years, then dating in the evenings. I guess the engagement seemed a natural progression. We obviously don't share the same faith or even moral standards. In the end, I don't know what we shared. So I guess I really didn't love him, in the happily-ever-after sense." She gulped. "Why do you ask?"

"Because I think I'm falling in love, Robbie." One of his hands rose. He tenderly brushed his knuckles against her cheek, then ran his fingertips gently along her jaw, stopping under her chin. "With you."

Her voice came out in a squeak. "But you barely know me." She barely knew herself. This past week had been a lesson in life like she'd never experienced.

"I know that. It doesn't makes sense, but it's true. Please tell me I'm not the only one who feels this way."

In a moment like this, Roberta couldn't handle staring back at her own reflection. As if he knew what she was going to do, he released her hands. She twined the fingers of one hand with his, just to keep touching him, and with her other hand, she plucked off his sunglasses. The swelling of his black eye made her wince in sympathy. Her heart twinged too, knowing it was her fault.

The bright sunlight caused him to blink a number of times until his pupils shrank to small black dots, emphasizing more of the dark chocolate brown of his eyes. Roberta stared into his eyes, thinking back over the past week, about how different he'd turned out to be than her first impression, yet in many ways, no different at all. Nothing less than a gentleman the entire time, he'd listened to her with the right mixture of sympathy and distraction as she poured out the story of her failure at the most important relationship in a person's life, and her poor judgment regarding Mike's character. His steadying influence had held her together when she needed it, and through his spiritual guidance she had managed to grow in spite of it. She couldn't help but feel the bond that had developed. But love?

She had thought she loved Mike, and that was the biggest disaster of her life. But Garrett was nothing like Mike. Mike used his power and influence as his father's son to intimidate people to do his bidding, where Garrett was a natural leader; his inner strength and quiet confidence left no question of his authority. Over the years of working with Mike, she'd grown used to him because she'd had to, as her supervisor and the future owner of the company. Familiarity had bred more than contempt. And she'd allowed it to happen out of weakness. She saw that now.

Nothing going through her mind and heart felt the same when she thought about Garrett. At first she'd tried to get rid of him, but within a few days, she had missed him when he wasn't nearby. When he wasn't talking for the sake of talking, which she now suspected he did to distract her from her troubles, she enjoyed his company more than anyone else's. It was a foregone conclusion she found him attractive. And when they prayed and worshipped together, she had felt a bond like no other. Was this love?

Above all, he had been totally open and honest with her, as she had been when they barely knew each other. She could do no different now.

"No," she whispered, barely managing to speak above the volume of the rushing water, "I don't know what this is, but you're not the only one who feels this way."

Whatever he said, and she suspected it was her name, was lost as his mouth descended on hers. The sunglasses nearly fell out of her limp fingers as the touch of his tender lips seared into her memory.

For such a large man, his embrace was tender and his touch gentle as he lifted his mouth, angled his head a little more, then kissed her again. Roberta lifted herself as high as she could on her toes, leaning into him, crossing her wrists behind his neck, his sunglasses barely dangling from her fingers.

He made a sound that rumbled deep through his chest and kissed her again and again. Her knees nearly turned to jelly when his hands inched upward, along her sides, over her shoulders, until he cupped her face with both hands, and gave her one more slow lingering kiss, ending with his lips suspended over hers and barely touching, while at the same time his thumbs gently rubbed her nape.

Slowly, she sank to rest her heels on the ground, burying her face in the center of his chest and slipped her hands around his waist. He held her firmly but gently, like she was the most precious thing in the world. His chin rested on the top of her head.

"I'm sorry. I have to be back on duty in an hour. We have to go back."

She backed up and offered him his sunglasses. Instead of simply taking them from her, he lifted them out of her hand with one hand, then slipped the fingers of his other hand between hers. After he slid the sunglasses back on his face, he led the way back, still holding hands.

The simple gesture demonstrated his sincerity like none other, both comforting and casual, yet understatedly possessive. In a word, cherished.

They walked hand in hand, in silence. There was no denying *something* had developed between them, but what was that *something?* If this was love, then it was a quiet comfort, riding side by side with an excitement deep inside, unlike anything she'd ever felt before. She tried to ask God for an answer, but she kept getting too distracted by the warmth of Garrett's hand as he walked beside her.

Or was this what it was like to be, as the classic phrase said, "caught on the rebound"? She'd often heard the phrase but never understood it. Now, here she was, walking through the forest holding hands with a man she had only just met, when a week ago she wore another man's engagement ring. And she'd just kissed him, too. Not just a friendly peck kind of kiss, but the kind that made a woman's insides melt.

A week. The thought echoed through her brain. What was she doing? Had she lost her mind?

The path widened to the opening onto the road through the campground. A week. They talked of love, and she'd known him a week. And on vacation, yet, not even a normal lifestyle setting. What was she doing?

She pulled her hand out of his.

"Robbie? What's wrong?"

Garrett's confusion nearly broke her heart. "I have to go to the bathroom," she stammered, and ran for the amenities building, leaving him standing on the gravel road, alone.

thirteen

Dressed in his uniform and ready to go back on duty, Garrett waited at the entrance to the campsite. It didn't take a rocket scientist to see something was wrong, and he didn't want to leave without talking to her. Ephesians 4:26 reverberated in his head. He couldn't let the sun go down on her anger, not that he thought she was exactly angry, but he couldn't let this go unattended. Time was too short.

He nearly laughed. Time? He'd known Robbie a week, but in that short week, his head and heart had been turned upside down. From the moment Robbie did a flip over his hammock, his heart had done a flip over her. But, he wasn't foolish enough to believe in love at first sight. Rather than diminish his initial attraction, the additional time spent with her beyond that only magnified it.

His heart skipped a beat, then restarted with a thud as Robbie entered the campsite.

"Robbie? Are you all right? Can we talk about it?"

Her face paled, and she shook her head. He opened his mouth to speak, but nothing came out.

"I can't talk now; I have to think. I'm sorry, Garrett."

He didn't like the sound of that, but she'd given him no choice. He would wait.

≈

Roberta busied herself at the campsite, trying to fill her mind with meaningless activity, and failed. The sight of Garrett back in his uniform did strange things to her insides. He was Mr. Ranger again. Tall, dark, handsome, dedicated to his job, committed to his faith in God. If his past performance was any indication, anything he committed himself to, he would pursue with equal unfailing devotion.

Beyond the shadow of a doubt, he meant what he said about falling in love with her. Now that she was away from him, she knew that she was in the process of falling in love with him, too. Would she be equal to his expectations? Could she be? According to Gwen, many women had wanted to be in her position. The fact that she was, scared her to death.

Before she drove herself into a frenzy, Gwen and Molly returned for supper. Busy discussing the rangers they'd met once again, neither Molly nor Gwen noticed how jumpy she was as they prepared their dinner. Molly blabbered on about the ranger who had teased her about her flaming red hair, and from the sound of things, they had exchanged phone numbers, with Garrett's recommendations.

To keep herself occupied, Roberta volunteered to take care of all the dishes after supper, while Molly and Gwen set up tarps, since the sky had clouded over. Diligently, she scrubbed every dish and glass meticulously until everything sparkled, which was difficult to do with plastic.

Seconds after Molly and Gwen excused themselves for a trip to the outhouse, Garrett showed up on his ranger rounds.

"Hi, Robbie." He stood beside her, waiting for her to respond. Not looking up, she rewashed one of the pots, trying to scrub out a black spot that looked like it had been there for years.

"Will you tell me what's wrong? Have I done something. . .?"

Roberta shook her head. "You haven't done anything wrong, Garrett. Please understand."

Noting the absence of retreating footsteps, she turned to see him not only still there, but with the dish towel in hand, drying the clean plates she had neatly stacked on the drainboard. His hand froze midwipe when he noticed her staring at him. "See? I'm a 90s kind of guy. I do my share of the housework, even in the great outdoors."

She nearly dropped the pot. "Aren't you supposed to be on duty, like, being Mr. Ranger?" she squeaked out.

"Please, don't hide from me, Robbie."

She buried her hands in the soapy dishwater. "I'm not hiding," she mumbled. "Things are happening too fast for me."

Garrett finished drying the last plate, then stacked it neatly with the others.

While helpless to protest with her wet sudsy hands, Garrett touched his fingertips to her cheek, then trailed them lightly to her ear as he brushed back a stray strand of hair. "Okay. You know where to find me."

Just as he did on the first day she met him, he straightened, touched the brim of his hat, and walked out of the site.

❧

Roberta stared into her bowl of soggy cereal, pushing all the matching colors into groups and patterns. Molly and Gwen watched her but fortunately didn't comment. Rather than go searching for the rangers with them, Roberta grabbed a half bag of stale bread and left for the nature trail. She'd seen more than her share of rangers.

With less enthusiasm than the last time she tried this, she sat in the same spot as a short week ago, absently feeding and taking pictures of nature's little creatures, thinking of the resident nature expert.

Being in close quarters, she actually had come to know him fairly well. She knew what activities he liked and didn't like, she knew about his family, his job, his interests. He was devout, honest and sincere, truthful to a fault, and tremendously loyal. Over and over, she listed his good and bad qualities in her mind, but she still had to be realistic. She'd only known him a week. A short week. She didn't believe in love at first sight. However, she'd known Mike for years, so that was no indication of knowing a person's character, either. She needed more help than her own experience could offer. She didn't know many verses by memory, but Proverbs 3:5–6 came to mind. "Trust in the Lord with all your heart, and lean not on your own understanding. In all your ways acknowledge him, and he will make your paths straight."

Roberta fell to her knees, alone in the quiet forest, and

prayed. *Dear Lord God. I'm so sorry I've pushed You aside. Now here I am, asking for help. I know I made a bad choice with Mike, but now I see that You showed me before it was too late, and I thank You for that. But what about Garrett? Am I falling in love with him? Is he the one You've meant for me? Please show me what to do. And I'll trust in You from now on, because You are God, the Master and Creator of all.*

Roberta scrambled to her feet, her mind clear. She had let her bad experience with Mike distort her budding relationship with Garrett. She didn't have to marry the man right away, she didn't have to marry the man at all, but she could get to know him better. If things progressed, God would direct her to know if the relationship was good and right. He'd shown her what a creep Mike was. He could also show her what a swell guy Garrett was.

Roberta threw the bread on the ground, scooped up her camera, and ran down the path, all the way to the camper. Garrett would show up sooner or later. He always did.

While she waited, she made idle conversation with Gwen and Molly, constantly checking over her shoulder, forcing herself not to jump to her feet every time someone walked by or a vehicle slowly drove down the road. Garrett did not appear to be making the rounds.

Supper was a tasteless affair of the last of their food and leftovers thrown together. Just before sunset, someone walked down the entranceway into the campsite, but even though she recognized the ranger uniform, it wasn't Garrett. Her heart sank. It was Molly's ranger friend.

Roberta grabbed her flashlight and headed down the road. If he wasn't going to come to her, she would go to him. She walked through the campground, sticking to the main road, turning her flashlight on as night started to fall. He was nowhere to be found. After more than a week of use, the white beam started to turn yellow. Roberta smacked the flashlight a few times, but it continued to dim, then went out.

She stood in the middle of the road. She could either go

back to the campsite, knowing he wouldn't show up, or go to the ranger headquarters, where he was doing whatever it was that rangers did. With the other rangers. If he was there.

Glancing both ways, Roberta started to hear little noises in the bush. Holding back a shudder, she walked quickly back to the campsite. She didn't want an audience when she talked to him. Besides, in the morning, being Sunday, she knew where she could find him.

&

At sunrise, Roberta awoke.

Molly snored away as Roberta tiptoed out of the tent trailer, using as much stealth as she could. Not wanting to arrive breathless, she walked down the road, onto the nature path, then chose the fork to the lake.

As she approached the clearing at the shoreline, she heard his guitar and his voice as he sang quiet songs of praise. When she could see his face, she noted he wasn't wearing his sunglasses, and his eyes were closed. Rather than intrude yet, she stood back in the bush and watched, thinking of what to say now that she was here.

His eyes opened as he changed songs, but Roberta remained frozen. Today his songs were different. While still reverent, it took her a while to realize the connection. He was singing songs of trust, expressing his confidence that God was in control, and giving God complete reign in his life. Then he stopped and laid the guitar on the blanket beside him. Instead of closing his eyes, he slumped, and buried his face in his hands to pray. Although he mumbled, she could still make out a few words, including her name and something about letting her go.

Roberta couldn't watch. She could no longer intrude on his private moment with God. She forced herself to walk away slowly and quietly, then once she figured she was out of earshot, ran the rest of the way to the camper and slipped inside, back into her sleeping bag. She lay there, her eyes open, staring at the top of the tent, until Gwen awoke.

Garrett did not show up for breakfast.

When all the dishes were done and put away, they started packing up the camper and taking it down, ready to go home.

Roberta couldn't remember feeling more depressed. For every stage that was taken down, she remembered Garrett's part in helping her set it up and, at the same time, the fool she had made of herself in front of him. Yet he had kept coming back. And now when she wanted him, he didn't. Her eyes burned as she took down Garrett's hammock.

Finally hooked up and ready to go, Roberta surveyed the campsite. This had been the best vacation of her life. She had a wonderful time, she had found herself—and true love. And lost it.

They drove to the dock, and Roberta helped heave the canoe atop Gwen's car. Just looking to the side where Garrett sat every Sunday morning caused her throat to tighten, nearly choking her.

Back at the site, they made one last check for forgotten articles, then drove away. As they cleared the park entrance, Roberta saw Garrett standing almost hidden by the trees, his arms crossed over his chest, watching. He didn't smile. He didn't wave. He'd broken her heart—or had she broken his?

It was over. It was time to go home and get on with life.

Molly chattered constantly the entire trip home. Dutifully, Roberta thanked her for providing a much-needed escape, and the chance to get her head together. As soon as she dumped her clothes on her bed, Roberta hopped in her own car to dash off and buy a few day's worth of groceries before the store closed. While she was there, she dropped her film off at the one-hour photo department so it would be ready when she was done.

When she picked up her pictures, a large envelope was attached.

A giddy teenage girl explained to her that she had won a free enlargement, but since Roberta did not answer the page, the clerk picked one of the photos to enlarge and told her if she wanted a different one, she could return it at no charge in exchange for a photo of her own choice.

Roberta wanted to go home, not hang around waiting for a picture. Being her camping pictures, she doubted she would need a 16 x 20 portrait of a stupid squirrel.

With her groceries sorted and put away, all that remained was the envelope of pictures on the table. First, she opened the large envelope to see her free enlargement.

Roberta sucked in a deep intake of breath as she pulled out a large photo of Garrett standing tall and erect, bare-chested, muscles flexed and ready, holding the large ax, poised to cut her firewood on the first day with him. Her brain froze as she stared at the photograph, bringing back with astounding clarity every event from when he backed the trailer into the campsite for her to the last sight of him as she left with Molly.

He had won her love without trying, by only being himself. Honestly. Naturally. And she had rejected him out of her own fear and self-doubts. By the time she admitted to herself what had happened, it was too late. She couldn't blame him. She'd behaved abysmally.

Instead of looking at the rest of the pictures, she lowered her head to the table and cried.

※

Roberta woke up in her soft warm bed at dawn. As much as she tried to sleep in, her internal body clock had not yet reset itself. Tossing and turning, she gave up, showered, and dressed.

She started to make herself a large pot of coffee, when a flash beside the stove caught her eye. In the corner of the counter, Mike's engagement ring lay where she had tossed it the day Garrett had been there. Just looking at the expensive trinket turned her stomach.

She opened the lid to the garbage can, ready to toss it where it belonged when the phone rang.

"I want my ring back," Mike demanded without any salutation or polite chitchat.

"You broke off the engagement; the ring is legally mine. And everyone in the office heard the whole thing, so try and take me to court over it."

"It's worth a lot of money. If you give me the ring, you can have your job back."

Roberta held the phone in front of her and stared at it, unable to believe what he said. According to what she heard with her own ears a few short days ago, Mike wanted more than just the ring before she got her job back. She hung up without replying.

The sparkle of the ring in the sunlight stopped her once more from tossing it in the garbage can. Holding it up into the sunbeam, she let the beauty of it catch the light. The ring was gorgeous, and she knew what it was worth. It would be a horrible waste to throw it out. She let the lid drop shut and dropped the ring into the bottom of her purse instead.

The second she touched the coffee can, the phone rang again. This time it was Molly, loaded with questions. "How are you, are you still upset, has Mike called, has Garrett called? Just checking to make sure you're okay." On and on.

After assuring Molly that she was feeling just peachy, she hung up. Everything she did made her think of Garrett. Seeing the ring made her think not of Mike, but of Garrett holding it in the light. Mike's phone call reminded her what slime Mike was, in comparison to Garrett's upstanding morals and un- selfish ways. Even her clothes reminded her of camping, which made her think of Garrett all the more.

She spent the day cleaning up and doing her washing.

The next day, she did the ironing and went out looking for a job.

The next day, she did the same.

All day, every day, she could only think of one thing. One person. Garrett. What was he doing? Where was he? What was he thinking? Was he wearing the sunglasses she had bought him? Was he thinking about her?

She depressed herself terribly.

Enough was enough. Roberta decided she had pined over Garrett too long, and it wasn't going to get any better. She drove to the mall, marched into the jewelry store, and asked for the manager, where she presented him with Mike's ring and the appraisal certificate.

She had no regrets selling it. The jeweler gave her a fair price on the ring, nowhere near what it was worth, but a decent price on a used ring. Now it could be a bargain for some couple somewhere who were truly in love.

After she made all her purchases, she still had plenty of money left over. Smiling, she patted her purse and headed home. She packed some suitable clothes, then left a message on Molly's answering machine not to worry. The second she hung up the phone, Roberta put her plant back in the kitchen sink and took off.

The hour-long drive to the campground was the longest hour of her life. When she arrived, she managed to pick a nice small private campsite. Emptying all the paraphernalia onto the ground, she was ready to begin, but quickly became overwhelmed. In her excitement, she hadn't realized the volume involved. The kind elderly man who owned Hank's Outdoor Store had had his staff load up the car for her, and now that she saw the stuff strewn about her feet on the ground, she couldn't believe the volume of goods necessary for a short camping trip. A lot of it she was familiar with from Garrett's family's camping accessories, but beyond that, she had no idea what to do with most of this junk.

And she had no idea how to set up her brand-new tent.

But she knew who she could ask.

She glanced upward at the position of the sun in the sky, then checked her watch. Garrett would have already started the afternoon presentation. Leaving everything as it lay on the ground, she headed for the amphitheater. Rather than disturb anyone by walking in late, she sneaked into a seat on the end near the back, where she sat and watched Garrett.

While he smiled at the crowd and presented his information in an entertaining manner, he lacked his usual enthusiasm.

In the back of her mind's eye, she pictured him sitting alone and dejected, praying beside the lake. And she knew it was her fault. Again.

At the close of his presentation, he followed his usual routine, asking if anyone had questions or comments, and politely if not enthusiastically answered every one of them. Finally, no more hands were raised.

"Is there anyone else?" he asked, scanning the crowded amphitheater for any stragglers.

Roberta raised her hand.

Garrett pointed to her. "Over there."

She stood and faced him across the little amphitheater full of people. She saw him flinch momentarily as he recognized her, and then he stiffened his posture.

"Yes?" he asked.

Roberta gulped and clasped her hands in front of her churning stomach. "This has nothing to do with your topic, but I do have a question, Mr. Ranger. You see, I'm not a very good camper, and I don't seem to be good at putting things together. I've got this tent and stuff, and I think I'm going to need your help."

They stared at each other as a hush grew in the crowd.

He had no comment.

She swallowed hard. "I miss you, Garrett. And I'm sorry."

Garrett's face paled and his voice trembled when he replied. "Don't do this," he said, barely loud enough for her to hear.

Roberta blinked hard. Her voice started to crack, and she didn't care. "I'm sorry," she repeated. "I do love you, Garrett."

"Robbie," he choked out. He clenched his hands into fists and rammed them into his pockets.

Tears welled up in her eyes, and she forced herself to keep them open. She knew everyone was staring, but she could only see Garrett, and he was fast becoming blurry.

All heads and eyes turned on Garrett as he stood at the front, constrained and ramrod-straight. She squeezed her eyes shut. She'd made a spectacle of him, and herself, too. This was not the way she had meant for this to happen. She'd botched everything from the first moment she saw him, and now she had embarrassed him in front of all these people.

Roberta turned to leave, rejected by his silence and lack of response. She clenched her teeth, determined not to run until she was out of sight of Garrett and the crowd.

Garrett called out, his voice choked. "Robbie, wait!"

He ran up the center aisle and through an empty section, jumping over some of the seats in his haste.

Very gently he touched her shoulder with his fingertips. "Robbie, nothing's changed. I still love you, you know."

She knew he meant it. It was herself she wasn't sure of.

"I love you, too, and I've handled this badly, but I need more time. Can we take this slowly? Can we, you know, date and stuff?"

Garrett bent his head, then brushed a lock of hair off her face. "Yes, I'd like that. But be warned. I intend to try my best to convince you to marry me."

She smiled and bit her quivering lower lip. "I think I'd like that."

"Robbie. . ." his voice trailed off, like he didn't know what to say. He tipped her chin up with his fingertips; the corners of his mouth curled up slightly. "Do you really have a tent that you need help setting up? You did this to come here to see me?"

She pulled off his sunglasses and gazed into the depths of his soft dark eyes, seeing past the purple bruising to the kindness of his soul. "Yes," she whispered.

Garrett's eyes glistened, but he blinked tears back, then smiled.

She opened her mouth to explain herself, but before she could say a word, he pulled her close until she was pressed against him from head to toe, held her tight, and buried his face in her hair.

Roberta opened her mouth to speak but gave up before she said a word. Any talking would have been drowned out by the thunderous applause around them.

epilogue

"Are you finished yet? How long have we been in this stupid duck blind, anyhow?"

Roberta slapped her thigh in frustration. "It's not a duck blind, it's a raccoon blind. And if there were any raccoons out there, they're gone now!"

"Robbie." In his cramped sitting position, Garrett rested his elbows on his knees and bowed his head to drag his hands over his face. "You're in credit and collections. You work in the accounting department. If the real photographer got sick, they should have found someone else to do this if they were running on a deadline, not you."

"Who? Mr. Mulderberry? I don't think his wheelchair would have made it up the hill, do you?"

"Robbie. . ."

"Oh! I know! Kathy! She's not due to have the baby for another week and a half. There's plenty of time left to do a photo shoot, right?"

"Robbie. . ."

Roberta waved the camera in the air, accidentally hitting him in the cheek with the strap. He barely noticed. "I suppose Joanie could have done it if she came back from the Bahamas a few days early from her honeymoon. She probably wouldn't mind."

He held his palms in the air toward her to silence her. "I give up! I know it's a small staff. I know you'll take some wonderful raccoon pictures for the magazine. This just isn't exactly my idea of what we'd be doing this weekend."

Roberta sighed and sagged. Neither had she pictured them huddled together under a musty canvas covering deep in the woods, trying to take pictures of a family of raccoons who allegedly were taking the ceramic statues out of a wealthy gardener's landscaping display and carrying them into the middle of the forest. She figured it was a stupid idea, trying to get pictures of them back at their den hoarding their treasure, but the owners of the magazine she'd been working for during the past year and a half thought it would be a great story, but only if backed up by photographs.

"This is your fault they stuck me with this," she griped. "Who else on staff is married to a wildlife biologist?"

Before she realized what he was doing, Garrett removed the camera from her hands and pulled her close. He nuzzled her cheek and gave her a gentle kiss. "Yeah, you are married to a wildlife biologist, and don't you forget it." He kissed her gently on the mouth. "Happy anniversary, darling. We'll go out somewhere special tomorrow."

Roberta smiled. She loved it when he called her "darling" because it reminded her of when they first met, and her thoughts that one day the woman Garrett called "darling" would be a lucky woman. She was, indeed, a lucky woman.

After nearly making the biggest mistake of her life, God had directed their meeting, their courtship, and now here she was, married to her Mr. Ranger.

Using just her fingertips, she touched his chin, then ran her hand slowly down his throat to rest in the center of his chest. Feeling the increase in his heartbeat following the path of her fingers, she smiled in feminine satisfaction. Instead of kissing him, she drew small circles on his breastbone, maintaining a short distance between them, enjoying his reaction.

ぷ

Garrett smiled at Robbie, sitting before him in her favorite camping clothes; her khaki slacks with one patched knee, her gray sweatshirt dotted with holes from stray campfire cinders, and the most disgusting pair of hiking boots he had ever seen. To top it off, she wore one of his Parks and Recreation hats, and as usual, it was crooked. The other rangers always laughed when they saw her wearing it.

He covered Robbie's hand with his own, pressing it against his chest, against his heart, where she belonged. He'd prayed for his perfect soul mate, and God delivered her.

"I love you, Mr. Ranger," she whispered.

With his free hand, he tipped her chin up, then leaned forward to kiss her. "And I love you too, Mrs. Ranger."

A Letter To Our Readers

Dear Reader:

In order that we might better contribute to your reading enjoyment, we would appreciate your taking a few minutes to respond to the following questions. We welcome your comments and read each form and letter we receive. When completed, please return to the following:

Rebecca Germany, Fiction Editor
Heartsong Presents
PO Box 719
Uhrichsville, Ohio 44683

1. Did you enjoy reading *Gone Camping?*
   ❑ Very much. I would like to see more books
      by this author!
   ❑ Moderately
      I would have enjoyed it more if _____

      _____

      _____

2. Are you a member of **Heartsong Presents**? Yes ❑ No ❑
   If no, where did you purchase this book? _____

   _____

3. How would you rate, on a scale from 1 (poor) to 5 (superior), the cover design? _____

4. On a scale from 1 (poor) to 10 (superior), please rate the following elements.

   _____ Heroine   _____ Plot

   _____ Hero   _____ Inspirational theme

   _____ Setting   _____ Secondary characters

5. These characters were special because_____
   _____
   _____

6. How has this book inspired your life?_____
   _____
   _____

7. What settings would you like to see covered in future
   Heartsong Presents books?_____
   _____
   _____

8. What are some inspirational themes you would like to see
   treated in future books?_____
   _____
   _____

9. Would you be interested in reading other **Heartsong
   Presents** titles?   Yes ❑   No ❑

10. Please check your age range:
    ❑ Under 18   ❑ 18-24   ❑ 25-34
    ❑ 35-45   ❑ 46-55   ❑ Over 55

11. How many hours per week do you read?_____

Name _____

Occupation _____

Address _____

City _____ State _____ Zip _____

Experience the joy of love...

Romance readers will love this brand-new collection of contemporary inspirational novellas, all centered on the season of spring. Includes the stories *E-Love* by Gloria Brandt, *The Garden Plot* by Rebecca Germany, *Stormy Weather* by Tracie Peterson, and *Bride to Be* by Debra White Smith.

400 pages, Paperbound, 5 ³/₁₆" x 8"

❤ ❤ ❤ ❤ ❤ ❤ ❤ ❤ ❤ ❤ ❤ ❤ ❤ ❤ ❤ ❤ ❤ ❤ ❤

❤ ❤ ❤ ❤ ❤ ❤ ❤ ❤ ❤ ❤ ❤ ❤ ❤ ❤ ❤ ❤ ❤ ❤ ❤

·····Hearts♥ng·····

Any 12
Heartsong
Presents titles
for only
$26.95 *

CONTEMPORARY ROMANCE IS CHEAPER BY THE DOZEN!
Buy any assortment of twelve
Heartsong Presents titles and
save 25% off of the already
discounted price of $2.95 each!

*plus $1.00 shipping and handling per order
and sales tax where applicable.

HEARTSONG PRESENTS *TITLES AVAILABLE NOW:*

(If ordering from this page, please remember to include it with the order form.)

Presents

Hearts♥ng Presents

Love Stories Are Rated G!

That's for godly, gratifying, and of course, great! If you love a thrilling love story, but don't appreciate the sordidness of some popular paperback romances, **Heartsong Presents** is for you. In fact, **Heartsong Presents** is the *only inspirational romance book club*, the only one featuring love stories where Christian faith is the primary ingredient in a marriage relationship.

Sign up today to receive your first set of four, never before published Christian romances. Send no money now; you will receive a bill with the first shipment. You may cancel at any time without obligation, and if you aren't completely satisfied with any selection, you may return the books for an immediate refund!

Imagine. . .four new romances every four weeks––two historical, two contemporary––with men and women like you who long to meet the one God has chosen as the love of their lives. . .all for the low price of $9.97 postpaid.

To join, simply complete the coupon below and mail to the address provided. **Heartsong Presents** romances are rated G for another reason: They'll arrive *Godspeed!*
